She tore away and hurried down the hill. "Leave me alone," she shouted when he followed.

"I can't!" he growled.

He strode to her and pulled her around, groaning at the lush sensation as her body collided with his.

"Jude!" she whispered in shock.

Tormented beyond reason, he took that open mouth in a deep and ruthless kiss, smothering her protests.

Childhood in England meant grubby knees, flying pigtails and happiness for **SARA WOOD.** Poverty drove her from typist and seaside landlady to teacher till writing finally gave her the freedom her Romany blood craved. Happily married, she has two handsome sons—Richard is married, calm, dependable, drives tankers; Simon is a roamer—silversmith, roofer, welder, always with beautiful girls. Sara lives in the cornish countryside. Her glamorous writing life alternates with her passion for gardening, which allows her to be carefree and grubby again!

A Spanish Revenge

SARA WOOD

SWEET REVENGE

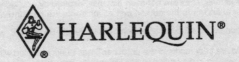

HARLEQUIN®

TORONTO • NEW YORK • LONDON
AMSTERDAM • PARIS • SYDNEY • HAMBURG
STOCKHOLM • ATHENS • TOKYO • MILAN • MADRID
PRAGUE • WARSAW • BUDAPEST • AUCKLAND

ISBN 0-373-80548-9

A SPANISH REVENGE

First North American Publication 2002.

PROLOGUE

GRIMLY Jude strode across the inner courtyard of La Quinta, quite oblivious to the lushness of the exotic planting and the cooling sound of the soaring fountain.

He was a driven man, intent on one thing only: justice.

For a whole month, he had done nothing but worry, eat and sleep by his father's bedside, first at the general hospital in Marbella, and then here, at home on their ancestral estate in a deep valley beyond the Sierra.

Of necessity, every last emotion had been focussed on the father who had loved and cared for him devotedly for the past twelve years since his mother had died when he was barely fourteen. His fury towards David Laker, the man who'd caused his father's stroke, had temporarily been put on hold. So, too, had his shock on discovering that Laker's daughter, Taz, had crawled into his heart and his bed on her father's instructions.

'Taz!' he ground out hoarsely, and stopped for a moment as a physical ache caught him unawares.

He squeezed his eyes tight shut, ruthlessly working on eliminating her image: a woman who was tall, shapely and naked, with skin as smooth as butter, dark eyes luring him into her outstretched arms with the promise of the most intensely erotic lovemaking he'd ever experienced in the whole of his life.

But she was no good. Her father's puppet. Without morals. He should be glad he wasn't tangled up with her any more, even if his body had a life of its own where she was concerned. Lust was natural. She was a very sexy woman and he'd been celibate for three months.

Ashamed of being diverted from his purpose, he moved

5

on, head bowed. Outside the door of Mateo's suite, he paused, steeling himself for what he would see. Then he knocked and went in. His heart constricted every time he saw his beloved father and this was no exception.

Once Mateo had oozed life and laughter, lighting people's lives with his enthusiasm and energy. But not any longer. The pale, shrunken figure on the bed lay motionless, the outline of the wasted body barely disturbing the smooth line of the cashmere blanket.

Jude swallowed and a profound compassion welled up within him. This was a man who'd been wronged. Laker and his daughter *must* be brought to book somehow.

Urgently he strode forwards, suddenly conscious that his own vigour and mobility must be painful for his father to bear. Tenderly, lovingly, he smiled at the twisted ruin of a face that had been altered out of all recognition by the massive stroke—the direct result of David Laker's ruthless betrayal.

The trouble had begun three months earlier when Laker had denied that Jude's father had been the main investor in Laker's private hospital. Sensing a possible scam, Mateo Corderro had immediately demanded a private investigation into the hospital's financial affairs.

The outcome had been totally unexpected. Just two months later the investigation had confirmed that there was no record of any such investment. Laker was vindicated and Jude's father had been branded a liar and a fraud.

Jude had been there when his father had received the news and had suffered the stroke. It was a moment he would never forget for the rest of his life. And now he was determined to find out how Laker had fooled the investigators so completely.

'Father!'

Mateo winked in acknowledgement. It was all he could do and that small gesture broke Jude's heart daily. His father, his own flesh and blood, was in a living hell, with his intelligent, active mind trapped in a terrible prison.

Gently Jude rested his hands on the bony shoulders. He embraced his father affectionately and with great care. Those shoulders had been powerful a short while ago, that chest broad and muscular. Rage ripped through Jude, almost choking him.

'I'm going to find Laker,' he said tightly. 'I'll find out how and why he cheated you. I give you my word!'

His father winked again. Unable to speak for the pity of it all, Jude clasped his father's hand and wished he could read the desperate message in the pained eyes.

'I'll call in later. Carmen is coming to read to you.'

Jude found a reassuring smile from somewhere, kissed his father's furrowed forehead and left his ageing nanny to continue the thriller she'd chosen.

He took the winding, hairpin road down to Marbella and cruised along the seafront to the neighbouring Puerto Banus.

'Laker!' he snapped in an imperious demand to the maid who opened the apartment door.

'He's not in!' she cried in alarm.

Jude snorted in disbelief and headed straight past her, flinging doors back violently on their hinges as he stormed through the vast penthouse, hunting down his prey.

'Laker!' he yelled. *'Laker!'*

And then he saw her. Taz stood at the top of the stairs, her hair mussed, her eyes red and swollen. Jude stood stockstill and stared at her, shaken by her appearance.

It was three months and two days since they'd last met. In that short time she'd changed beyond all recognition. The once slender and beautiful woman who'd stolen his heart was now bloated, her face white and puffy, her clothes shapeless and ugly.

Taz inwardly flinched at Jude's stunned appraisal. She knew she looked dreadful—but he'd done this to her. Since he'd coldly announced they were through, her days had become filled with eating and crying and now she hated herself for allowing him to ruin her life. But she loved him so much… Dear heaven, how she loved him!

Miserably she edged down the stairs, gripping the gilded banister for support. She pushed past him in to the sitting room, but Jude followed her and she turned to face him. His dark eyes were glinting with such a fierce hatred that it chilled her to the bone.

'Get out!' she said in a low, shaking voice. 'Leave before I call the police!'

'Where is he?' he hissed, a furious energy emanating from every pore.

'Out!' she flung at him in relief. 'Out of the country!'

Jude let out a muttered curse and clenched his fists, clearly frustrated. 'Then he's a coward. He must have known I'd come for him.'

'You took your time,' she pointed out coldly. 'It's a month since the investigation. He could hardly hang around waiting for you to turn up to air your grievances—'

'Grievances?' Jude roared, his voice cracking with emotion. 'Have you any idea what's happened to my father—?'

'I don't know and I don't care!' she broke in furiously, hating to see his hostility, desperate for him to go.

He rocked on his heels as if she'd hit him. 'I don't suppose you do,' he said in a harsh whisper.

Of course she cared. She'd been fond of Mateo. But he'd tried to bring her own father's integrity into disrepute and she could never forgive him for that. 'If your father's been shamed, then I'm sorry but he should never have claimed he'd financed my father's hospital. It was downright dishonest!'

'You're wrong! We've been through this!' Jude grated.

Taz despaired. They both believed their fathers to be in the right. She *knew* that hers had told the truth when he'd denied all knowledge of Mateo Corderro's supposed investment. And the facts had confirmed her belief.

Jude's claim was ludicrous. Why did he persist in defending the indefensible?

Struggling to believe his father, against all the evidence, had taken its toll. Jude looked terrible: thin and drawn, his cheekbones standing out starkly in his hollowed face. Fierce lines had appeared between his brows and the dark shadows beneath his eyes suggested he'd slept fitfully for a while.

Her heart ached for him and she knew she still loved him. But his very courtship of her had been a sham, a means of learning enough facts about the private hospital so that his father could make his story ring true. Why couldn't Jude admit that?

'Jude,' she began jerkily, 'I know that family honour is important to you and I admire you for sticking up for your father, but—'

'David Laker has cheated and lied and my father's life is in ruins,' he persisted. 'Maybe he's evaded me for now, but I won't rest till I've paid Laker back for what you've both done—'

'Me?' she gasped indignantly. 'I'm totally innocent in all this!'

Jude exploded. 'Innocent, hell! You can't deny that you were the honey-trap, to encourage my father to invest! *Dios!* How could he do that with his own daughter? Your father virtually stripped you naked and planted you in my lap!'

Taz's mouth fell open in astonishment and anger. Not for the first time did he marvel at her acting ability.

'What? *Me?* A—a *honey*-trap?'

'Spare me the protestations,' he muttered scornfully. 'You talked of little else but the hospital. You sold it to me and I, like a fool, carried your enthusiasm to my father who put the best part of his fortune into it because it was such a worthy cause. Worthy! Run by a charlatan and a thief! You both deserve to rot in hell! I'll clear my father's name if it takes me the rest of my life!'

'This is stupid!' she stormed. 'There's no evidence—'

'I have my father's solemn word and that is all the evidence I need! He is a man of honour and integrity. Your father is nothing but a cheap little crook with ideas of grandeur—'

'How *dare* you?' she gasped. 'It's wonderful that he wants to use his fortune to provide a specialist clinic—'

'Money laundering, that's what it is!' Jude's nostrils flared. 'He hasn't got a noble bone in his body. There's talk that he came to Spain because he was on the run from the law!'

'What? I will not let you insult my father out of sheer pique! Get out, you vicious, twisted *liar*!' she yelled.

As though the strength had seeped from her body, she sank into a capacious settee, one flailing arm sending a standard lamp flying. He fielded it and set it straight, his anger so intense that his hand was trembling.

'I can't get out of here quick enough!' he flung viciously. 'But you haven't seen the last of me!'

'For your own sake, Jude,' she persisted desperately, 'you must accept that the solicitor has denied witnessing your father's signature. There is no record of any transfer of funds to the hospital account—'

'It went to a holding company—'

'Which doesn't exist!' she cried impatiently. 'Rumour has it that your father had been shelling out money for business deals which failed, and that's why he was broke, not because he'd risked every penny he had on my father's venture.'

'The only business deal that went wrong was the one with David Laker,' he said coldly. His eyes narrowed. 'I will prove it to you. I won't forget this. I don't care how long it takes but I will have my revenge! You have my solemn word on that!'

CHAPTER ONE

Six Years Later

BALANCED precariously on one leg and clasping her bruised shin, Taz suppressed a groan of pain and stared in dismay at the mess in front of her.

One coffee table had been up-ended, scattering everything on it: a vase, now broken; flowers from the same, now dripping; a smashed mug and a bag of sweets, which was merrily soaking up the remains of her hot, strong coffee.

Tornado Taz strikes again! she thought moodily. How did things like this happen? No one else had arms and legs that behaved like windmills when they were put under extreme stress.

Her heavy lashes fluttered down over pained dark eyes. She waited for the wave of nausea to subside, indifferent to the chattering coming from her phone. Only she had a body that sometimes became a dangerous weapon and had people running for cover. When her emotions got the better of her, perfectly normal arms and legs turned into missiles and just one wilful hand could clear an entire mantelpiece.

But she had good reason for her clumsiness this time. Apart from the fact that it was just four months after her father's death, she was soon to leave her apartment in Madrid *and* her beloved nursing job *and* all her friends, to live with her stepmother Belinda in Marbella. On top of

11

that, Belinda had announced some startling news over the phone.

'Guess what?' she'd said tremulously. 'I—I have a lover, Taz!'

At the time, Taz had been standing next to a vase of flowers, which, mysteriously, had gone flying into the air. Lurching forward in an attempt to catch it, she had cracked her shin on the low table and had ended up with her body jackknifed in agony as objects had hurtled in all directions.

Sublimely oblivious to this drama, her stepmother had chattered on with strange intensity. 'Darling, he's gorgeous! Charismatic, witty, sexy...'

Adjectives had poured relentlessly into Taz's left ear. Wincing with pain, she'd hooked the phone between chin and shoulder then she'd rubbed her screaming shin through the huge ladder in her black tights.

'Hold on a minute!' she interrupted when she found her voice again. 'Did you say you have a *lover*, Belinda?'

'*Have* I just!' The slightly manic tone wobbled a little. 'One...one who's young and knows how to have *fun*!'

'That good?' Taz suppressed an understandable pang of envy.

'Sheer heaven, darling! He's bursting with life!'

Taz made a face. That sounded like unintentional criticism of Taz's late father, and it was typically tactless. Poor Bel. She must have found it hard when he'd suddenly shown his age in the last few weeks before his death.

But...a lover! Taz frowned, not sure how she felt about that. It seemed a little too soon for her stepmother to play the merry widow. After three years of marriage, wouldn't a longer period of mourning have been more seemly?

She felt immediately contrite. That was horribly prissy! She was acting like a crabby old spoilsport. Nevertheless, it might be just as well that she'd soon be able to keep a friendly eye on Bel's interests—not that she was much better than Bel at assessing character!

Her most spectacular mistake had been in believing Jude Corderro's sweet-talk. Her father had often told her she was far too willing to see a person's good side, and when Jude had turned out to be a conniving rat instead of the lover she'd dreamed of all her life she'd realised he was right.

Still suffering the fall-out from her traumatic affair with Jude, Taz had tactfully left home on her father's third marriage and had found a nursing post in Madrid, spending just her holidays at his luxurious penthouse apartment. It had been an odd situation. Determined to be independent, she had lived on her pay as a staff nurse. Her father's apartment, however, was in Puerto Banus, which was known as Marbella's golden mile, and it boasted the highest per capita income in Europe.

Naturally, the area attracted hangers-on like flies to rotting meat. As David Laker's widow, Belinda had inherited half the Laker fortune—Taz receiving the other half—and suddenly her beautiful stepmother had become a great prospect for any ambitious male.

The bonus prize would be her father's exclusive private hospital, with its state-of-the-art technology and highly paid consultants. As a route to prestige, power and social acceptance, any association with the hospital would always be coveted by social climbers.

'How long have you known this guy?' Taz asked with justifiable suspicion.

'Six weeks,' Belinda replied. 'I was lonely and started partying again—and there he was on this gin palace of a yacht.'

'With eyes only for you!'

'Er...yes. Yes!'

She'd been lonely, thought Taz with a qualm. How awful. Belinda must have begun the relationship shortly after the last time Taz had visited.

'I should have come to see you more often,' she apologised, riven with guilt.

'You've had your head-cases to look after,' Bel said with rare understanding.

Taz ignored the blunt description of the patients in the intensive care unit of her neurological ward, and continued feeling remorseful.

'I neglected you. I could have broken my contract and moved in with you straight after Dad died,' she said humbly, using her instep to hook the coffee table onto its feet.

But Belinda wasn't listening. Fulsome praises were being heaped on the new lover's head and Taz became aware of a striking change in her stepmother. The sullen, listless woman of the last few months might sound over-excited, but there was a brightness in her voice too, as if an immense depression had lifted from her shoulders.

'I never thought I'd find anyone again at my age—'

'Your age!' Taz exclaimed. 'You're thirty-two, not ninety—!'

'My looks are going. I've got lines—'

'You're gorgeous. Anyway, I've got lines and I'm eight years younger than you!' declared Taz.

Thoughtfully she jammed the receiver between her chin and shoulder then bent her long body in a supple movement and began to mop up the pool of water with her handkerchief. Whilst down there, it occurred to her that Belinda had probably rushed into this affair purely because she'd been lonely and insecure. That wasn't surprising, considering Belinda's background.

She walked over to the entrance to the kitchen. 'It's early days,' she cautioned, aiming the sopping hanky and newspaper at the sink, and missing. Grumbling to herself, she wandered back to the coffee table and stuffed the mimosa and orange-blossom into the mug as a temporary measure, absently popped an unscathed jelly baby into her mouth and straightened up. 'Just take this relationship slowly,' she advised indistinctly, chewing on the glutinous sweet.

'You're joking!' Belinda shrieked. 'He's a dynamo fitted with turbo boosters. I've been swept off my feet! Everyone thinks he's *fab*. A sort of...Pierce Brosnan. Walks like he's oiled! Dances like a dream—and he adores shopping if you please!'

Taz felt alarmed. He sounded horribly like a gigolo from a 1930s movie. She bit the jelly baby in half and wondered if he had a moustache.

Belinda was very vulnerable—and Marbella was full of vultures on the look-out for rich women and juicy pickings. Plenty of men seemed ready to sell body and soul for the benefits of a designer suit, wrap-around sunglasses and the chance to chirrup *'ciao'* at minor celebrities.

Playing for time to work out how to handle this situation, she commented noncommittally, 'Dancing and shopping! Very continental!'

'That's because he's Spanish.' Belinda yawned. Taz had the impression the yawn was from an excess of dancing and shopping rather than from boredom about her subject. 'He's the athletic type. Macho, strong and madly wealthy,' Belinda said, as if reading off a checklist.

With that last reassurance, Taz's tense mouth relaxed and assumed its normal, sweet expression as she smiled in fond understanding. Understandably, her stepmother was terrified of being poor again and she needed the security of money as badly as she needed the emotional shelter of a man's arm.

'Every woman's dream. What does he do?' she asked companionably.

'Spends money on me, *liebchen*! He's hugely generous. And *mucho* energetic!' Bel declared, irritatingly following the trend of the international smart set and sprinkling her sentences with foreign words.

Taz knew this was an attempt to fit in with people around her. In private, Bel was shy and down-to-earth. Why, then, was she putting on an act now? 'Bel, be straight with me—'

'I am!'

There had been alarm in Bel's tone. 'Then why—?'

'Questions, questions! I'm tired, Taz! We go to so many parties that I hardly see the morning.' She yawned again. '*Quel hombre!* And you'll never guess the people I've rubbed shoulders with—!'

'I haven't time to! I've got to cut you short,' interrupted Taz hastily. The call to Marbella would go on for ever if Belinda embarked on a list of celebrities and criminals in exile who fetched up at parties! 'I'm just going on night duty—'

'So am I, darling!'

To her surprise, Taz felt extreme distaste at that suggestive remark. She didn't know why. Belinda had a right to a sex life.

'Bully for you!' she managed without conviction. 'But I can't gossip now. Give me a blow-by-blow account when we meet. I finish work tomorrow night, then they're throwing a farewell bash for me the following day. After that I'll go straight to the airport. You said you'd leave your car for me?' she added hopefully.

'Well, I'm not having you embarrass me by arriving in some rust-bucket of a hire car!' declared Belinda. 'I don't need mine. I have only to snap my fingers and I have my own hunky chauffeur at my beck and call.'

'Sounds keen as mustard,' commented Taz, feeling worried again.

Belinda paused, then said, her voice a little shaky, 'So— so he should be! I'm quite a catch!'

'You certainly are,' said Taz slowly.

'Anyway, he'll drop my keys at the information desk for you. I'll be out when you arrive, so let yourself in.'

'Oh.' Even the most obtuse person would have heard the disappointment in Taz's voice. 'I thought you'd be at the flat,' she said forlornly. 'It's my first night, Bel. Start of my new life—'

'I know, darling, but we can celebrate any time. Jude's promised me a romantic dinner on his yacht.'

The world seemed to come to a shuddering halt. Jude. *Jude!*

The name sucked the breath from Taz's body, leaving a roaring in her ears and an emptiness in her stomach. Horribly shaken, she sat down so suddenly that she almost missed the seat, banging her bottom on the hard edge before she managed to slide back till the rungs of the chair connected with her rigid spine. The urge to be sick was overwhelming.

'Jude?' Beneath the smooth navy skirt, her knees trembled uncontrollably, but she jammed her vertebrae into the rungs to give her mind something else to complain about and said tinnily, 'Th-that's an unusual name for a Spaniard!'

Don't let it be, she pleaded in a state of total panic. She hung onto the phone with both hands in fear. Please, she begged fate, chocolate-coloured eyes glistening with angry tears. Not him. Not Jude—with Belinda!

She dug her teeth into a trembling lip as she waited

while her stepmother gushed on interminably. Taz's heart rate rose like a rocket. There must be more than one Jude in the world, she reasoned, trying to be sensible, even if there was only one conniving, lying, cheating, callous…

'Cute, isn't it?' Belinda was very much on a high. 'It's short for Judeo—like Taz is short for Tasmania.'

Taz gave a strangled gasp. The receiver fell from nerveless fingers and hit the wooden arm of the chair with a clatter. Appalled, she frantically snatched it up and jammed it against her ear, just in time to hear the terrible confirmation from the extraordinarily self-absorbed Belinda.

'So everyone calls him Jude. *Jude Amador Corderro.*' There was a long silence then, jerkily, she said, 'Isn't that music to your ears?'

More like a heavy thud, Taz thought in horror, now seriously alarmed for her stepmother's well-being. This was terrible! She must say immediately that Jude was an out-and-out con man and an absolute *louse*!

She opened her mouth to denounce him but, before she could, something less noble tried to emerge. Into her heart and mind and body surged a sickening, visceral jealousy which made her want to screech down the phone at Belinda and tell her to keep her hands off him, to stop shopping, dancing, bobbing about on yachts…oh, God, *everything*!

An image of entwined naked limbs flashed into her mind, torturing her by replacing the petite Belinda with her own tall, more lavish body.

Taz's sooty-lashed eyes closed in self-loathing, but the vision persisted with a brutal intensity. The beautiful Jude was the kind of man who devoted his whole being to love-making. She knew that with every cell in her entire body. And each one of those cells was cruelly communicating

with her brain, reminding her of that undeniable fact so
forcibly that she had become hot and fully aroused for the
first time in six long years.

It was a lifetime ago. But, unbelievably, this unwelcome
warmth, this delicious glow, was all for him. She hated
the man like poison—but still her breasts were thrusting
painfully against her uniform and there was a frightening
eagerness about her whole being as if she was anticipating
Jude's touch.

She couldn't believe it. Apparently her physical hunger
was more powerful than all those humiliating memories of
rejection and the extreme animosity she felt towards him.
Disgusted, Taz pressed her free arm against her chest re-
sentfully as if that gesture might return her breasts to their
normal, decent indifference.

Anger blazed in her dark eyes. Jude had cast a shadow
over her entire life. Since she was a small girl she'd always
longed to fall in love and to have a fairy-tale wedding and
had planned it down to the last detail. Then Jude had
crossed her path, raised her hopes, and dashed them again.

Several men since then had been keen to make her
dream come true but, to her dismay, every boyfriend had
compared unfavourably with Jude in the arousal stakes.

An irritable frown drew her dark brows together. It baf-
fled her why she seemed sold on Jude's slick and practised
technique when she could have had love and sincerity from
any one of a dozen, willing suitors.

And, every time another relationship had bitten the dust
because her heart had remained unmoved and her passion
had refused to be ignited, she had roundly cursed Jude
Corderro for the legacy he'd left her.

Somewhere in the background, Belinda was burbling on,
but her words were almost drowned by the furious beating
of her own heart.

Jude, she thought irritably, wasn't worth a moment's thought.

Jude... Topping her five-nine by four inches, dark, exciting and as unpredictable as a gypsy—yet sleek and groomed, like one of his Arab stallions. The kind of mouth you wanted to kiss the minute you set eyes on its humorous, quirky lines. Eyes...

Oh, stuff his wretched eyes, for heaven's sake! she seethed, gritting her teeth in fury. What if he *was* physically perfect? It meant nothing if his heart had been dipped in concrete. The man was a plausible liar who belonged in the sewers with the rest of the rats!

Her mouth curled in scorn. He had a con man's ability to make any woman believe she was the sexiest, most desirable female in the world. His ploy was to discover a woman's likes and dislikes and then to give her whatever she wanted: perfumed roses in her case, long walks to remote beaches, constant eye-to-eye contact as if the rest of the world didn't exist...

Those eyes, admittedly, had been mesmeric. Almost black, sublimely capable of melting a girl's resistance with just one sizzling look...

What was she doing? She'd been cured of him. Definitely. Shocked by the emotions his name had awoken, Taz swept Jude's lingering looks to the back of her mind and tried desperately to concentrate.

'Then we went into Ralph Lauren and he bought me this fabulous...'

She listened to Belinda's happy chatter cynically. So he was *shopping*, was he? What a fraud! Jude didn't like shops; he abhorred them! This wasn't a 'boy meets girl, falls passionately in love' scenario. He was up to something. She froze, a neatly manicured hand going to her mouth in horror.

Jude could be settling an old score, just as he'd promised.

An all-pervading chill spread through the depths of her body despite the warm sunshine flooding her small apartment. She began to shake.

Cutting across Belinda's description of some divine shoes with handbag to match, she said abruptly, 'You're very vulnerable at the moment; be careful, Bel.'

'We *are* careful!' Belinda replied with a throaty chuckle, totally misunderstanding.

An excruciating stab of sexual jealousy came from nowhere. *'Belinda!'*

'Don't be disapproving, *cara*! I'm…I'm in love!' Belinda said expansively. 'I've never felt like this before. I'm deliriously, wonderfully happy!'

Taz shuddered. Love! This was worse than she'd imagined! Somehow she kept back the anger and the panic which were threatening to make her blurt out the truth about Jude. Belinda had to be treated with great care. She was fragile and easily hurt.

Oh, how awful! Taz thought helplessly. Jude would happily destroy David Laker's widow if he could! Should she tell? Perhaps not on the phone—that would be too cruel…

'But…you can't know much about him!' she protested with a heavy heart.

She knew so many things. The lies behind that slow, sexy smile. The heart-stopping absorption of his face when they'd made love… She groaned, infuriated at the way her mind was remembering only the pleasure and blocking out the pain.

'…and he likes the same things as me,' Belinda was saying with a hint of defiant tears. 'He's given me a platinum credit card. That shows he wants to pamper me and make me happy, doesn't it?'

'Wow! Platinum!' exclaimed Taz, hastily backing down. What on earth was she to do? Weaning Belinda away from Jude and his platinum card would be a nightmare! 'It's a very generous gesture,' she said with as much warmth as she could muster.

But she wondered whether Jude had become rich by lawful or shady means. He'd acted corruptly once; what if that had become a habit? It would be disastrous if Bel unwittingly became mixed up with Marbella's thriving underworld.

Hearing from Belinda in lurid detail about his 'bed-me' eyes, heavenly kisses and the dear little hollow at his throat was just sickening. Any minute now, she'd lose all control and say what a poisonous jerk he was.

'Bel,' she said firmly, 'I've got to go to work. See you at your apartment.'

Fortunately, Belinda was too engrossed in her own affairs—affair—to pick up on Taz's hoarse tones.

'I must dash too, *chérie*. I've got someone on the other line and I'm only half in and half out of my Valentino. *Ciao*, darling. Mwah, mwah. Oh!' she squawked suddenly. Did I tell you we…we're s-secretly engaged?' There was an expectant pause. 'Hello? Hello? Taz—the line's gone all crackly. Are you there?' she cried in panic.

Taz covered her mouth so that Belinda couldn't hear her rasping breath any more. She was gripped by such a deep sense of shock that her whole body had become unnaturally still. Now she knew Jude's hidden agenda. He wanted to scoop the jackpot: the David Laker Hospital itself.

If he married Belinda he'd have her—and thus the hospital—virtually in his pocket. Taz stared bleakly into space. He'd persuade her stepmother that he should take an active part in managing the hospital—and that would mean she and Jude would attend meetings and face one another across the boardroom table. Impossible, unthinkable!

'*Taz!* Say something!'

'I'm here,' she answered weakly.

Unwanted came a picture of Jude carefully selecting the ring, proposing, slipping the ring on Bel's finger, kissing her into submission, making uninhibited, crazily passionate love...

Her heart lurched with an agonising pain. How dared he? The man was unbelievable! How could he latch onto the defenceless Belinda? How could he behave so spitefully? This vendetta was nothing to do with Bel and yet she was being used for Jude's revenge.

Taz started. Belinda was yelling in her ear. 'What? Sorry I—'

'I *know* your father's not long dead, but I—I *must* marry Jude. Say you're glad, Taz! I couldn't bear it if you deserted me! I'd die if you weren't my friend!' wailed Belinda almost hysterically.

Making a huge effort, Taz pulled herself together and spoke calmly, anxious to soothe the touchy, needy woman who'd always been desperate for unconditional love and affection.

'Idiot! Of course I'm not deserting you!' she said with gentle affection. 'I'm...overwhelmed. It's such an unexpected surprise. You...' For the sake of her stepmother, Taz gritted her teeth and said *almost* what was expected of her. 'You must both be very happy.'

'We...' Belinda gave a little sob. 'What do engaged couples normally feel?' she said jauntily. But there were tears in her voice.

'Dear Bel, why are you upset? You sound odd,' Taz cried in concern. 'Is something wrong—?'

'No! Nothing! I told you, I'm a bit tired, that's all.'

And very agitated. Taz frowned. She was very emotional. 'Have an early night,' she suggested, practical as ever.

'Can't! Jude insisted on taking me out.'

Taz's strong brows arced even closer together. Belinda sounded almost scared of him, as if he was running her life and dictating terms. She wondered if he had already moved into the penthouse suite—and if the three of them would all be tucked up cosily together, having jolly breakfasts. She couldn't bear to live with them if that was the case.

Jude would be looking appealingly tousled and unshaven as he emerged from the bedroom where there would be abandoned clothes and sheets hanging off lampshades and curtain rails as evidence of his extraordinary sexual energy and inventiveness.

Taz winced, her thoughts winging to the evening. She imagined the two lovers coyly murmuring that they must have an early night. She saw herself putting some very loud flamenco on the CD player to drown any noise and feeling a right gooseberry as the action in the bedroom hotted up. Well, she wouldn't stand for it. She'd live elsewhere.

'Has he moved in?' she asked bluntly, interrupting another eulogy.

'No! It wouldn't be right. He's going to marry me!' Belinda said primly.

'Oh.'

Perhaps they weren't even having sex. That was better—no, worse, if he respected Belinda that much. Taz felt confused.

'So you must wear decent clothes when you come here, and not show me up. *Compris?*' Belinda was babbling. 'The residents in Puerto Banus will die if you arrive in your usual slops—and Jude hates women who don't take care of themselves. He doesn't mind at all if I spend a whole day at the beautician's. You take understatement too far, Taz! Do tidy your hair—and wear something with a label, darling, or I'll wither in shame. Must fly. *Adios!*'

A label. All her stuff had labels, Taz thought in exasperation as she hurried to change her laddered stockings. Everyone had labels. How else did you know how to wash stuff? As for tidying up, well, she'd intended to travel comfortably, wearing... OK, her slops—jeans and a T-shirt.

But...her heart did a quick pit-a-pat. With Jude hovering around impersonating a film star, she suddenly had an overriding urge to look gorgeous: something on the lines of a sleek goddess from the pages of a fashion magazine. She'd warn him off Belinda, and all the while he'd be kicking himself for treating her so brutally...

Taz gave a wry smile and cursed herself for her vanity. How insecure and despicable and utterly shallow! But... She grinned. How satisfying!

A tug of war developed in her mind. She had no need of him or his admiration. Why should she make an effort?

Because she wanted him to be stunned into silence. Because her final memory of him was of his disgust as his scornful gaze had raked her huge, bloated body. And she'd howled her eyes out when he'd gone because it had been he, and he alone, who'd turned her into a mockery of the slim, carefree and happy girl she once was.

Taz sighed. Vanity had won hands down. Any woman would understand. The urge to look fabulous was too strong to deny. It amounted to a heartfelt need to salvage her wounded pride.

So she ignored her worthy outburst of common sense,

grabbed her bulging bag and tipped out the contents, frantically checking that her new gold card was in her wallet.

Eventually she found it glued to a boiled sweet and gazed at them both in grim satisfaction. Her father's complicated finances were still being sorted out, but it had amazed her that once the bank manager had known she'd inherited half of her late father's private hospital he'd removed the frown from his face and flung credit cards, offers of loans and financial assistance at her.

She'd suddenly become a valued customer. Now that she had money—or the prospect of it—she was allowed to run up huge debts without being chased for payment! Taz's eyes gleamed. Since she had the overdraft facility, and would soon have real cash to go with it, she might as well get a twenty-four-year service!

Starting with her hair. She studied herself critically in the tarnished mirror on the back of her flat door. Yes, her hair was unruly. Like her. She gave a rueful smile. Her Spanish mother had a lot to answer for! Taz knew that her passion for life—and love—could rule her brain if she didn't keep a strict hold on herself.

Since she was intending to be cool and controlled, that mocha-coloured mop ought to be tamed into something more sophisticated and smooth. Plaits were definitely not sophisticated, nor worthy of a fashion mag.

Then there was the problem of what she'd wear for this memorable meeting. Ignoring her nurse's uniform, she imagined something chic and understated skimming her too lush body. And high heels were a must—frivolous ones, to point up the fact that she didn't need to catch buses. They'd bring her up to Jude's height too, so she could look him bang in the eyes as she delivered her stinging salvo. Taz beamed at the prospect.

Make-up next. She peered at herself critically. Her

brows were too dark and thick, needing an attack with the
tweezers. As for the rest... She frowned. How did you turn
a pleasant, ordinary face into that of a woman with razor-
blade cheekbones, inner serenity and confidence?

Experimentally she sucked her cheeks in to see the effect and decided to wear a hat with a brim and be mys-
terious.

On the way to work, she got herself into a state about
the colour of her prospective outfit. Blue, she decided, was
too gentle and would evoke a sweet innocence she didn't
want to project. Black would be too severe—and smacked
of insecurity. Red...too come-and-get-me, potentially
tarty. Frantically she eyed women on the metro. They were
wearing black, grungy olive and beige. Safe but dull. No
help there.

In the middle of mentally running through every colour
in the spectrum, Taz realised what she was doing and sub-
sided, ashamed of herself for being so pathetic. Why was
she so hell-bent on impressing Jude, a one-time lover she
hadn't seen since she was eighteen?

A small frisson of pleasure lit up the memory banks in
her body. Despite all her efforts, she could feel herself
soften and become drowsy with sensuality. The Spaniard
next to her immediately identified her body language and
submitted to the personal challenge by chatting her up. She
passed him her soggy bag of jelly babies with a kind but
subtly rude suggestion and grimly concentrated on thwart-
ing Jude.

Almost certainly the silver-tongued charmer intended to
go through with this farcical marriage. Only then could he
get his hands on Bel's inheritance. Taz fumed at his sly
tactics. She had to stop him—but how? Women in love
were renowned for never listening to criticism.

And she knew that if she told Jude to sling his hook

he'd only laugh. Any opposition would reinforce his determination—and she'd be risking a rift between herself and Belinda.

Increasingly alarmed, Taz entered the hospital and hurried towards the lift, deep in thought. Jude's strength and confidence and sense of humour must have seemed the perfect replacement for the father-figure Bel had always searched for.

Up popped the handsome, silver-haired image of Taz's own father, whose powerful character and enormous charm had initially captivated the fun-loving Belinda despite the gap in their ages.

David Laker could persuade anyone to do anything. His parties and his business acumen were legendary. Had Belinda missed that fire and energy, the non-stop action and extravagant compliments?

Jude was clever. The son of a con artist, he knew how to play whatever part necessary to get what he wanted. So he'd deftly turned himself into Bel's husband-substitute, lover and fellow shopaholic... And now they were having *fun* together. They were laughing, creasing up with the giggles perhaps, sharing private jokes and developing a bank of shared, happy memories.

Her footsteps slowed, her eyes glittering with anger. It hurt to know he could enjoy another woman's company more than hers, however stupid that resentment might be. And it appalled Taz that she should be so jealous.

But, worst of all, the man she'd idolised was turning out to be an even more vile ratfink than she'd believed possible. That misguided loyalty towards his crooked father was driving him to enter a loveless relationship. To him the sacrament of marriage apparently meant nothing and he didn't give a damn that he would hurt someone in the process.

She drew in a rasping breath. Her chest hurt with the agony of it all. Extraordinarily, she'd once loved this worthless piece of dirt.

'Taz, are you all right?'

She blinked. 'Fine. Onions for lunch and last-shift blues,' she said, quite truthfully, to one of the English nurses on her ward.

And she'd *make* it fine. She'd find a way to stop him. Jude would soon be a mere blip in her life, and, more importantly, Belinda's. Fine. Sorted.

'Let's get cracking,' she said briskly.

It wasn't long before everything was quickly wiped from her mind except the welfare of the patients in her section. When she was nursing her clumsiness disappeared—even when her emotions were engaged. Her warmth and affection flowed towards the sick and frightened and downright bad-tempered and yet she never had an accident, dropped their notes or bungled an injection.

As the case conference proceeded and the day staff went through each patient's medical status, it became clear to her that she'd miss her work. Leaving was going to be a terrible wrench and she certainly didn't want to become just a co-director of the Laker Hospital with Belinda.

'I draw a vast salary,' Bel had said airily. 'All I have to do is sweep in for coffee and attend the occasional finance meeting where I sign whatever they put in front of me. Piece of cake.'

Taz had immediately felt some misgivings about emulating this vague approach to directorship. Now she was on the brink of abandoning all her training, she suddenly knew how much it meant to her. Nursing was her passion, the be-all and end-all of her life.

The conference ended. Moist-eyed with affection that this was her last shift, Taz went to see each of her patients.

Holding the hand of an elderly man with frightened eyes who'd undergone a serious operation, she calmed his fears.

'Of course you're not going to die!' she said warmly. 'Neither side would have you, in those blinding orange pyjamas!'

And the man laughed, life and humour irradiating his strained face. Taz giggled with him and adjusted the strap on his oxygen mask, noting that his heart rate had stabilised. She'd judged him right. Patients, she could handle.

A great love spread through her, warming her heart and bringing a glow of joy to her strong-boned face. She wouldn't let her inheritance change her life. Once she'd given Jude the heave-ho, she'd find herself a nursing job at the Laker Hospital and they'd increase the percentage of charity cases they took in.

Taz heaved a relieved sigh. Everything would be OK, she just knew it.

CHAPTER TWO

THE farewell party had gone on longer than she'd antici-
pated. She hadn't realised how popular she was, and the
compliments and presents had overwhelmed her so much
that she'd knocked over the hired waiter, a vast tray of nib-
bles and two glasses of champagne to gales of affectionate
laughter.

Laden with excess luggage, she'd only just caught the
plane. Flinging herself and an enormous toy giraffe into the
seat, she wriggled down her fashionably brief skirt and
leaned back in dizzy delight.

Her head buzzed from the noise and the lethal cocktail
invented by one of the doctors. Her feet hurt from running
in the ridiculous high-heeled sandals and she was pink from
exertion and the wolf whistles she'd attracted.

But she felt a million dollars. Succumbing to vanity had
been a great idea!

The suit of uncrushable champagne linen—and the wisps
of matching silk underwear beneath—felt gorgeously sinful
and made her look graceful and willowy. A fine foundation
covered her Mediterranean complexion, and a glossy nude
lipstick seemed to have produced a wildly provocative pout
to her mouth.

As for her hair...! Taz couldn't believe her tousled waves
could look so sleek. Gleaming like dark, liquid chocolate,
her hair had been parted centrally and drawn in a classic
sweep to the nape of her neck where it had been tied in a
glamorous chignon with a huge scarlet silk bow.

Fantastic! she'd thought in amazement, when she'd added
a wide-brimmed natural-straw hat and ruby-red earrings.
And after the party the male staff in particular had hugged

and kissed her goodbye with unusual enthusiasm, eagerly inviting themselves over to see her during their holidays. It was enough to turn a girl's head, she thought in amusement.

Almost super-confident and impatient to meet Jude to see his reaction, she fidgeted all through the flight. Yet she experienced a sudden invasion of bungy-jumping butterflies in her stomach when she picked up Belinda's flashy open-top sports car from the airport.

Nervously she drove the silver monster along the notoriously dangerous Carretera Nacional to Marbella. It was almost midnight and the tourists were on their way back to their hotels and holiday flats. However, the evening was just beginning for anyone with Spanish blood and the town was in party mood.

Slowed by the bumper-to-bumper traffic, Taz joined the dawdling procession of poseurs, fending off constant male invitations and practising her aloof-princess look for when she met Jude.

A short distance away in Belinda's exclusive penthouse suite, Jude grimly emptied yet another bottle into the sink. 'You don't need this,' he insisted irritably, one powerful arm carefully holding back the hysterical Belinda. 'If you feel stressed out, then come to me for support instead! I'm here for you now. I don't want you drinking in secret.' More gently, he said, 'Can't you see what this stuff is doing to you?'

'I don't care! I do need it!' she sobbed piteously. 'I forgot to tell you—Taz is coming any minute now. I'm scared that she'll find out about our arrangement and go all moral on me!'

'*Taz?*' Shocked beyond belief, he spun around, eyes blazing. 'Taz? What the devil did you ask *her* for?' he roared, too anguished to hide his reaction.

'She asked herself!' Belinda wailed.

He groaned and raked a hand through his hair, trying to

wrench his feelings into order again. These days he was so much on edge that the slightest problem disturbed him more than it should.

He was juggling with too many people's lives, coping with their emotions and needs and denying himself any time, any space. His father was increasingly giving cause for worry. Each day he saw him he seemed older, frailer, more sunken into himself. Time was running out. His father was dying and family honour—so vital to any Andalusian—had not been satisfied.

Jude could hardly bear to see his father's hopeful eyes. Sometimes he imagined they were accusing him of failing in his filial duty. Whatever the truth, the pressure to clear his father's name was immense.

And in Belinda he had found the solution.

'We're going out tonight,' he reminded her stiffly, trying to rein back his agitation at Taz's imminent arrival. 'We agreed that we ought to be seen in public together as much as possible.'

'I know. That's OK,' she said, her mouth sullen. 'I told her I wouldn't be here to meet her.'

Bel had no thought for others sometimes. He cursed softly under his breath. They'd have to get rid of Taz quickly. She mustn't interfere in the perfectly civilised arrangement he'd made with Laker's widow.

'I know you don't love me,' Belinda had said a week ago in that frank way of hers. 'But I need a strong man around me, someone to lean on—and you've been like a rock since David died. Will you marry me, Jude?'

He'd been so astonished that he'd hesitated, perhaps some part of his younger, romantic self longing for a woman he could cherish and love with all his heart. But past experience had told him that was unlikely and he certainly had no desire for emotional turmoil. His life held enough of that already.

For days he'd been wrestling with his conscience. He

knew she'd come to rely on him and, in all truth, he'd expected his seduction of her to take longer.

Before he'd met her, his intention had been to make her as happy as possible, but to marry her at all costs. That decision had been taken in the cold light of day following his father's bout of flu which had left him pitifully weak. He'd vowed to do anything to give his father peace of mind.

Even marry a woman he didn't love.

Yet, after deliberately engineering a 'chance' meeting with Laker's widow, he'd been touched by her vulnerability and had spent hours comforting her and trying to raise her spirits. It seemed that she'd really loved the old reprobate.

To his surprise, he'd enjoyed her company when she was sober. She could be sweet and funny and he'd felt more like an elder brother to her than a prospective husband. His lack of passion worried him, but she seemed content with his restraint.

She wanted security; his aim was to gain control of the hospital—though she was unaware of that fact. It wouldn't be a marriage of great passion, but he'd become fond of Belinda and she seemed to care for him. The marriage made sense for both of them and they'd discussed the future with equal enthusiasm.

She'd blossomed, suddenly full of joy. He felt better about that. At first it had been easy to give her pleasure, and he'd done everything he could to provide her with the fun and diversions she craved. Underneath, when she forgot her airs and her affected mannerisms, she was gentle and trusting—but when she hit the bottle she became a different person.

Only an hour ago he'd realised how seriously addicted she'd become. When he'd tried to talk to her rationally about the alcohol she consumed, she'd flown into a rage. He had searched the apartment and had been appalled to find that she'd hidden bottles everywhere. She'd gone berserk when he'd begun to dump their contents.

And now Taz was on her way! Was it any wonder he was

on a short fuse? He wouldn't be able to face her without a row ensuing. He gritted his teeth.

'If Taz is visiting, I'll get out of your way for a few days while she's here,' he said shortly. 'But I don't understand why you need Dutch courage to face her.'

'Because she's beautiful and successful and everybody loves her. I said I'm madly in love with you and she's *not* visiting, she's coming to *live* here and I'll have to keep things *tidy* and…and not have a drink whenever I want one!' Belinda yelled miserably.

'*Live here? Permanently*, you mean?'

She nodded, clearly scared by his reaction, her blue eyes wide and filled with tears. 'Does it matter?'

God, yes! If she knew… Holding back the threatened torrent of words that clamoured in his head, he released an exasperated sigh. 'I would have liked to know,' he said tightly. 'We could have discussed the problems this raises, having someone around who might notice I'm *not* head over heels in love with you.' Unable to contain himself any longer, he said curtly, 'Just give me a moment.'

Amazed at his restraint when, inside, he was choking with horror, he stalked out to the balcony. In the warmth of the night and to a background hum of chatter and the slap of waves on the hulls of the million-dollar yachts in the marina ahead, he forced himself to confront the worst scenario he could imagine.

Taz would move heaven and earth to stop the marriage. If she succeeded, his beloved father would abandon all hope and…

Sick to the stomach at the thought of the awful consequences, Jude passed a damp and shaking hand over his forehead, desperately fighting back his fear for his ailing father's welfare. Failure at this stage would be devastating. He dragged his white teeth over his full bottom lip, refusing to face the prospect.

He had to salvage the family honour. Laker and his

daughter had destroyed his father's health and, for a time, his standing in the community. Taz must not be allowed to rob them of their chance for justice.

Anger now glittered in Jude's near-black eyes as he stared out across the marina, his churning emotions receding behind a hard, cold determination. Behind him he heard Belinda pouring herself a drink from some hidden source. His heart contracted and he felt, suddenly, that his future was bleak, where once it had seemed everything he'd wanted.

What a hell of a hole he'd dug for himself, he thought, and wondered why the news of Taz's arrival had affected him so much.

And then he heard the unmistakable sound of Belinda's car. His jaw tightened as his urge to protect his father became a steely determination. He was more than a match for Taz. She was without morals and he'd make sure Belinda knew that Taz and her opinions weren't to be trusted. And with hatred in his heart he waited tensely for his first sight of Taz in six years.

Pleased she'd arrived, Taz gave a cheery smile to the security guard at the gate to the apartment complex. He waved her on with the enthusiastic leer of a man who thought he'd be in with a chance if only he had ninety million pesetas in the bank.

She parked the car then remained seated in it, her palms clammy with nerves as she wondered how she should greet Jude when they eventually met. Coldly? With polite charm?

This needed finesse. Belinda must be protected. She felt a familiar cloud of worry steal over her. Increasingly her stepmother had exhibited worrying mood swings.

They had been bad enough in the past, but seemed worse now. Sometimes her father hadn't been able to persuade Belinda out of the master bedroom to act as hostess for his parties. Later Bel might have emerged, bright-eyed and spar-

kling with happiness, only to sink into a deep depression
when everyone had gone.

Taz reached for a chocolate bar and bit into it thought-
fully. Perhaps Belinda was highly strung, like a racehorse.
It seemed to take nothing at all to send her into hysterics.
Well, it was her job to be her stepmother's rock.

Feeling confident now, she slid from the car, startled by
the excessive amount of shapely, tanned thigh on show beneath the minimal skirt. A fashionable girl could catch cold
frequently, she thought wryly.

He saw then that she was licking chocolate from her fingers
and an unexpected pang of desire seared right through his
body as he remembered the times she'd proffered her cho-
colatey hand and he'd solemnly taken each slender finger
and sucked it clean. It had been corny and sentimental, but
mind-blowing. And then they'd made love, the sweet, rich
taste of chocolate still lingering on her lips and inside the
moist warmth of her mouth.

'Devour me,' she'd said huskily, her eyes drowsy with
desire.

And he had, inch by inch of that sublimely flawless skin,
teasing, tormenting, and revelling in her uninhibited response.

Shaken by this deeply sensual memory, he watched her
bending to retrieve something in the car. His hands tightened
on the balcony rail because he could almost feel her firm
body as his gaze roamed hungrily over her neat rear and
feminine curves. And he knew, with a sickening truth, that
his future was no longer certain or clear-cut.

This wasn't what he'd expected at all. She'd set his carnal
instincts on red alert and that was the last thing he wanted.
Helplessly, he watched, raging against the lust that gripped
him with every dip and sway of her incredibly lush body.
And he hated her all the more for appealing to his base
instincts.

*   *   *

Taz rummaged in the bowels of the car, finally yanking the giraffe out from beneath her bags of presents. She emerged pink-faced and laughing at the animal's ridiculously long lashes and lolling black tongue.

'Come on, Graham,' she chuckled, christening it with the most unlikely name she could think of, 'let's find you somewhere to live.'

Hastily she finished the rest of the chocolate and licked her fingers then cleaned them meticulously with her handkerchief, hoping the residents weren't watching her dreadful behaviour with disapproval.

Nonchalantly she slanted a quick glance at the stepped-back building. No shocked faces peered at her from the windows but... She held her breath.

A man dressed all in black was watching her from the floodlit penthouse balcony eight floors up. Belinda's balcony. Something sharp hit her in the solar plexus and she didn't know if it was fear or surprise.

Quickly adjusting the brim of her hat to exclude the oddly menacing figure from view, she felt the thudding of her heart against Graham's soft rump.

'Graham, meet Belinda's vulture,' she muttered under her breath.

The confrontation had come sooner than she'd expected.

The man disappeared. Another one rushed out from the entrance and started unloading her luggage.

'*Numero veinte,*' she told the porter, glad she wasn't going to meet Jude with three suitcases and twelve carrier bags dangling from all points of the compass.

Her breath was high in her throat. Outwardly cool and composed, she adjusted a dainty strap on her sandal, picked up her highly fashionable bag and strolled into the building with Graham. While her luggage zoomed up in the porter's lift, she loitered in the atrium, guessing that Jude would want to meet her here rather than risk being denounced in front of Belinda.

She thought grimly that he must have been panicking at the prospect. Good! She'd make him squirm.

In the far corner, beyond the gilded statues and alarmingly well-behaved jungle—complete with waterfall and tropical birdsong—she could see the downward progress of the lift.

Graham squeaked. Taz found that she'd been crushing him unmercifully. She unpleated the wrinkles on her brow, arranged a regal smile on her face and began to walk briskly across the vast marble floor, her heels tapping like demented woodpeckers. The lift doors opened.

Grudgingly she had to admire his carefully staged entrance. It was worthy of a star performer appearing on Broadway. Framed by the lift's shiny steel interior, the glowering Jude waited a second or two for the full impact of his presence to be felt before he strode out.

And she was impressed, even though she'd tried to maintain a casual indifference. He was everything she remembered—and then some more. Dark, devastatingly handsome, and burning with a fierce, male confidence.

He wore a black shirt, artfully opened to display that irritatingly dear little hollow at the base of his dark, satiny throat, which she had kissed so often and with such pleasure. That was her stepmother's prerogative now. Taz felt a tremor run through her and easily eliminated it by thinking of his cruelty.

Almost calm again, she surveyed him in detail, noting that the black designer jeans sat low on his hips and that they were tight enough to show off his perfect, muscled rear and long, sinewy legs. Very macho, very Hollywood! Taz thought scornfully. But sexy, she had to admit, and she had to put a stern hold on her outrageous, wandering thoughts.

Searching hopefully for signs of ageing or decadence in his features, she noticed one or two small changes in his appearance. Now the set of his jaw and the grim lines of his mouth suggested a greater toughness and a hint of ruthlessness. This was a man to be reckoned with. She quailed. He'd be a difficult opponent, she thought. Then she remembered Belinda's needs and rallied.

Her head came up and she met his gaze boldly. Not surprisingly, Jude looked incredibly angry. His glittering eyes were fixed on her with unwavering intensity and Taz could see how women might fall for this brooding, bad-boy approach. Even she was having difficulty in avoiding the urge to quiver and mumble incoherently and her clothes seemed suddenly too tight.

But she was a trouper. Brooders could be made to laugh, bad boys disconcerted by sunny good humour. Good invariably wins over bad, she told herself optimistically, picturing herself as an avenging angel in gleaming armour, and Jude as a horned devil complete with tail and attendant rats.

'Jude!'

She flung her arms open in well-rehearsed delight, the giraffe dangling by one ear and incongruously shuddering from her sudden gesture. Jude blinked at Graham's lolling tongue in dumbstruck silence. Pleased at her small victory in winning back the high ground, Taz took the advantage, continuing in English because it gave her the edge.

'Well!' she trilled. 'It *was* you peering down at me like a little old lady twitching her net curtains!'

Clearly offended by her wicked comparison, he scowled and tightened his smooth-as-satin jaw. Taz gulped but mentally polished her armour and stood her ground.

'I was surprised. I'd only just heard you were on your way,' he stated, clipping out each word like a pistol shot.

'I can see what a shock that must have been,' she conceded, amused.

A shadow dulled his eyes and, for a moment, he looked as if he'd just seen hell from the inside. Startled, Taz realised how much he loathed her. Graham dropped to her side and dangled forlornly from her trembling fingers.

'Bel said she'd forgotten. I would have preferred to have

known earlier,' Jude replied icily, looking down his patrician nose at her. 'We'd planned an evening out.'

'On the balcony?' she teased, merry eyes dancing.

He wasn't amused. Tight-lipped, he said with studied deliberation, 'I went out for a breath of air.'

Liar, she thought. He'd probably recognised the sound of Bel's car and had rushed out expecting to see a podgy lump emerging. She hoped he was surprised.

Her lashes fluttered as she shot him a quick glance to see if he'd noticed the change in her. Apparently not. He was just scowling and looking at her as if she'd crawled from the gutter. She might as well have saved herself the trouble and worn her slops!

She cheered herself up by reflecting that he must have been hopping mad to know she was coming to live in Puerto Banus—worried, too, about what she might do about his engagement. Her spirits rose.

'And then you saw me! So you flew down to greet me!' she sighed. Then it came to her. That was just the tone to take with him! She'd be charming—and get in a sly dig or two! Fizzing with delight, her smile was more genuine when she said, 'It's lovely to see you!'

She stuck out her hand. He took a quick step back and looked at it with a frown darkening his face, as if she might be an expert in martial arts and intended to throw him on his back. If only! she thought in amusement.

'I assumed that under the circumstances you'd be hostile,' he said curtly, pushing his hands in his pockets and not giving her the chance to display potential black-belt qualifications.

'Hostile?' Curbing a terrible desire to add *'Moi?'*, she made a little laugh instead and looked perplexed. 'But I'm thrilled!'

And indeed she was. This would be her chance to clip Jude's wings and to teach him a lesson. Maybe in future he'd think twice about preying on weak women.

Filled with crusading strength, she moved forwards, grabbed a rock-hard arm and, secretly marvelling at his tense muscles, flung a few air kisses in the direction of his face. She felt glad that Graham was acting as a barrier between them because she didn't want body contact at all. Jude seemed horribly stiff, as if someone had just taken him from a freezer.

Despite that, Taz felt the temperature rise, and knew instinctively that it was because they were kissing-close. She was appalled to find that her old attraction for him had been re-ignited. A power surge of electricity from Jude's tautly held body was weighting the air between them with a heady sexuality and turning her legs to water.

She flashed him a quick look and almost gasped at the smouldering darkness of his eyes. Her breath left her lungs in a rush at that naked, carnal invitation. He hadn't changed, she thought tremulously. Uncontrollable passions still drove him.

She shivered. Unpleasantly startled by erotic memories, she moved back, cocking her head to one side and smiling maniacally, determined not to be affected. The stakes were too high to weaken. He *had* to be thwarted.

'Did you say...thrilled?' he repeated, his disdainful mouth back in the freezer.

Taz desperately added a soppy expression to the smile. 'When Belinda said who she was dating, you can imagine I was amazed!' she chirruped. 'But I only want her happiness. Why,' she exclaimed, revving up to an awful glee, 'you'll be my *step*-stepfather! Isn't that fantastic?'

Jude looked at her in undisguised horror. Then it was hastily *dis*guised behind an implacable expression. Taz felt immensely proud of her tactics.

'She's told you we're engaged?' He frowned. 'I can't believe it! I *told* her to keep it—'

'Quiet,' she finished drily. Naturally it would suit him to

marry in secret! 'Not anxious to keep your plans secret from Bel's friends, are you?' she hazarded airily.

For a split second Jude struggled to answer, and Taz congratulated herself on taking the wind out of his sails.

'Why would I want to?' he fielded with commendable smoothness.

Easy. So that her friends didn't dissuade her from such a stupid action, Taz thought cynically. She smiled and shrugged.

'I'm sure you would have your reasons. But now the secret's out we must tell everyone. I love weddings. We must give you both a huge do. Bridesmaids in purple, your bride in layers and layers of cream taffeta with lots of bows and an enormous train and you...' she eyed him speculatively '...you'd look fantastic in eighteenth-century costume,' she said with a suitably dreamy expression. 'Pale blue satin frock-coat, ruffled cravat and knee breeches—'

'Any marriage of mine will be a quiet affair, not a tacky show with Regency bucks and their doxies,' he drawled.

Taz's smile managed to include a smidgen of smugness. 'Quiet? With me and Belinda organising it?'

His dark eyes flashed an unmistakable warning. 'Quiet. Sepulchral,' he added. 'She said that she would go along with whatever I want.'

She almost gasped at the way the statement had been ground out between his teeth. Like hell she will, buster! she thought angrily.

'That's what all men believe,' she said, enjoying the chance to patronise him. She wagged a finger, to add emphasis. 'You're not married yet! If you want to keep your bride sweet, you'll have to let her have her head. And you do want her to stay dazzled by you, don't you?'

Jude surveyed her intently, his expression one of profound suspicion. 'What do you mean by that remark?'

She opened her eyes wide. 'You love her! You want her to be happy!'

His mouth slammed shut. He should have agreed, but apparently even habitual liars found some things hard to say. Taz despised him.

Purposefully, she tucked her arm in his and began to move him back into the lift. He wasn't putting up much resistance. She'd probably flattened him with the dual prospect of purple bridesmaids and knee breeches.

'I'm thinking...' she mused '...six pages. In navy satin, white lace collars and ballet pumps.'

Jude came to a standstill and she couldn't budge him. Her sideways glance told her that he didn't like the idea of pages, satin or ballet pumps. His face was like a stone.

'Over the top, Taz,' he said coldly. 'In a big way.'

'OK. Make it three pages, then. Children look so sweet at weddings,' she said fondly. And, delighted by his evident horror of domesticity to come, Taz ignored the warning signs and gave a sentimental sigh. From under the brim of her hat she peeked coyly. 'Speaking of children, I expect we'll hear the patter of tiny feet from your direction soon, won't we?'

There was a sharp intake of breath and Taz marvelled at the shudder that shook his body. He looked very pale.

'We haven't discussed children,' Jude bit out, retreating further into Arctic territory.

'You must! I know you adore them. Four's a nice number. One after the other, so they can all play together.' He made a strangled sound and Taz bounced on regardless, having a ball. Clearly he hadn't thought of the consequences of marriage. Well, she'd spell them out for him! 'I can see it all,' she said dreamily. 'You and Belinda pushing a buggy with a clutch of toddlers at your side, their little nappies drooping around their chubby dimpled legs—'

Her friendly arm was abruptly detached from his with such force that she staggered. A swift glance in his direction told her he was finding it difficult to restrain his temper. She felt a momentary flicker of fear when she saw that his chest had inflated and his shoulders were aiming for the atrium's glass dome.

'You're pushing your luck,' he grated. 'Stop it, Taz. I know you're having me on.'

His eyes gleamed and she knew he'd got her measure. But it didn't matter. He needed telling.

'But I have a word of warning.' She paused for effect, her expression suddenly solemn.

'Warning?' he growled, his eyes narrowing alarmingly. 'Now what are you up to?'

Taz took a step back, thoroughly intimidated. If he ever knew, he'd eat her alive.

'Heavens, Jude! No need to jump down my throat,' she persisted bravely. 'As your future step-stepdaughter I want our little family to be happy. You need to be aware that there's always a downside to having kids. There's the sleep deprivation, lack of a social life…'

She stopped, confused by the look of pain which flickered across his face.

'Leave it, Taz,' he said hoarsely.

All her instincts were telling her to ease up on him. But he didn't deserve her sympathy. Judging by his reaction she was on to a winner and, if she persevered in spelling out what marriage entailed, he might decide the game wasn't worth the candle.

'You ought to know these things. I know it sounds ghastly but Belinda believes that parents should look after their own children,' she persisted. 'It's because she was farmed out as a child when her mother had to work. You're aware that she was very poor?'

Frowning, Jude shook his head. 'I know nothing about her background. I certainly wouldn't have guessed she'd ever been strapped for cash.'

Taz stared. He was very uncomfortable with that knowledge, almost at squirming level. She wondered why.

'She had a terrible childhood,' she told him soberly, deliberately pulling no punches. 'Bel never knew her father—and her mother…well, it's not for me to say. It's up to Bel to tell you what profession her mother followed.'

Jude's face tightened. 'I get the picture.'

Taz worked on his heartstrings again. 'She's always been lonely. When she came home from school she had to fend for herself—'

'Are you exaggerating again? She speaks well.' Frowning, he folded his arms across his powerful chest and viewed her with frank scepticism. 'Dresses well.'

Taz nodded. 'Her first husband did a Pygmalion on her. He turned her into a society hostess. Ask her about it—there's worse, I swear.' Jude must know that he was dealing with an emotionally scarred woman. 'You have to believe me, Jude,' she finished passionately.

'I do.' He was clearly moved. 'It explains why she's so insecure. I've told her she's as good as—better than—most of the people she knows. But she's nervous of saying or doing the wrong thing. Poor Bel. Now I understand why she—' He broke off.

'Why she what?' Taz prompted.

'Nothing,' he said dismissively. 'Just something that suddenly makes sense to me.' He thought for a moment. 'My guess is that this husband bullied her and made her feel inadequate.'

Taz was surprised at his perception and the unwitting softening of his voice. 'You're right,' she said in relief, hoping that he'd begun to see Belinda as a real person instead of a means to an end. 'You see now why she would want to care for her own children. It'll be OK if you both take turns getting up in the night,' she finished, remembering she was supposed to be putting him off marriage.

Jude inhaled irritably, inky eyes glinting with suppressed anger. Taz suddenly realised that he didn't dare to annoy her in case she spilled the beans about him and his father.

It gave her almost unlimited power. She turned a high-wattage smile on him.

It had an odd effect. He virtually flinched, his hard, washboard stomach contracting as if she'd landed a punch there. And then his eyes blazed in fury.

'I see no point in discussing something that's in the distant future and which doesn't concern you,' he growled. 'Don't interfere, Taz!'

He was magnificently dangerous, snarling like a cornered tiger: fierce and threatening even in defence. Barely breathing, Taz clung to Graham, stroking his soft coat in an attempt to lower her adrenaline levels.

Jude's antagonism made her want to turn and run. Or lie down in surrender. Neither of those would help much. She had to goad him, push him to see that a loveless marriage would be too big a price to pay for revenge.

'The distant future could be closer than you think. Bel adores children,' she pointed out as she got to grips with the conversation again.

'So?'

'You need to get going quickly if you're to have a large family.' And she finished that off with a naughty wink.

Jude's eyebrow hooked up in response. Slowly, his brooding gaze ran over Taz's generous curves, lingering unbearably on each breast in turn with such telling intensity that it felt as if he'd touched her with his fingers. Pointedly he appraised the swell of her hips and flicked his gaze back to her hot face.

'Make love, you mean?' He let that thought roll around between them for a while and there was a dangerous air about him. 'Like...now?'

Taz was thrown off her stroke by the warm sexiness in his voice. And confused by the muddled feelings his suggestion evoked. She certainly didn't want Jude to rush up to the apartment and...and... She reddened. Her impulsive remarks had taken her further than she'd meant to go. As usual.

'Well, I—I wasn't...' Her voice tailed away. 'You're teasing me!' she complained.

'Am I?'

His velvety drawl caused havoc within her. She was so aware of him that her skin tingled as though his fingertips were working their way over every inch. The pressure built up in her chest as she stared at him, appalled by the vividness of her memories and her subsequent reaction.

Graham squeaked, saving her, and they both looked at him in surprise.

'Taz, why exactly are you carrying that thing?' Jude murmured.

She grabbed a scrap of breath from her collapsed lungs and croaked, 'Because it can't—'

'Walk,' he provided languidly, a faint cynical amusement in his dark eyes. 'Ask a silly question...'

Taz's face paled. They'd often finished one another's punch lines in the past. They'd laughed a lot together, done some daft things and had been so utterly happy that she'd never suspected for a minute that it had been an act on his part.

A cold shiver went down her spine. That sounded exactly what he was doing with Belinda: sharing fun things. Knots twisted in her stomach. He really was the vilest man she'd ever known.

'I'm not a cuddly toy sort of person normally. It was a present,' she said unnecessarily.

'Boyfriend?' he murmured, reaching out a lean, tanned hand and absently dead-heading a nearby hibiscus. The action puzzled Taz. When she met his gaze again she saw that his eyes were pinpoint-sharp.

Suddenly sad, she looked away, thinking of the men who'd loved her—good men. Men she'd lost because of Jude's legacy.

Her misty eyes focussed on Graham's velvety ears as she struggled for something pithy to salvage her pride. 'Boyfriend?' she replied merrily. 'Heavens, no—giraffes are far too knock-kneed for my fancy!'

Briefly, Jude's eyes twinkled with unexpected humour. His mouth widened for a second or two into a smiling curve and she found herself mesmerised by its sensual curl before she remembered that her stepmother had been kissing it.

'With those lashes—and especially that tongue—it's got to be female,' he pointed out drily.

'Oh, dear! And I've called him Graham!' she countered in mock dismay, ignoring his insult to the female race. Jude disconcerted her by struggling to suppress his amusement, but he was clearly grinning behind his hastily raised hand. 'Why can't it be masculine?' she protested. 'Men have long lashes. You...' Her voice tailed away. His lashes could bat for England but she didn't want him to think she'd noticed. 'You coming up to see Belinda with me?' she amended ungrammatically.

'Later. I think there are a few things you and I must discuss first. I thought we'd have a little chat together in the tapas bar here.'

She blinked, her senses spinning. He was virtually purring, and devouring her with his dark, gypsy eyes as if she would be a likely conquest.

Taz fumed. So much for being engaged! He didn't have a faithful bone in his body. Bel would be an emotional wreck if she married him.

'A chat? About the wedding, you mean?' she asked pointedly.

'About...you and me.'

Taz felt a small tremor run through her. He seemed to have the ability to tap into her sexuality with that husky inflection and the hint of intimacy. Jude had sex appeal in spades. Most men hadn't a clue.

Feigning the slow dawning of understanding, she swallowed to lubricate her parched throat and hazarded, 'Oh, you mean our relationship! Me being your step-stepdaughter?'

Clearly annoyed, Jude shot her a cynical glance. 'About us knowing each other in the past. I haven't told Belinda that we were lovers.' There was a long pause during which she became increasingly agitated at the images flashing through her mind. 'I don't want to hurt her,' he said throatily. His eyes narrowed. 'Have you said anything?'

Taz heard the edginess in that query and shrugged her elegant shoulders. 'Whatever for? I haven't even told her I knew you. There seemed no point. It was just a kid's thing,' she said offhandedly. 'Experimentation,' she added for good measure. 'Came along with the obligatory spots and the rush of hormones...'

'You missed out on the spots, Taz, but the hormones certainly rushed about. It wasn't as casual an affair as you make out. As I recall,' he mused, softly reminiscent, 'our relationship reached seismic activity for a while. I know the earth moved for both of us.' He saw her opening her mouth to make a defensively flip reply and forestalled her drily. 'And, before you say so, it wasn't anything to do with earthquake tremors or nearby quarry-blasting.'

Infuriatingly, he'd read her mind and her intention as if they were still close and operating like two people merged into one. That shook her almost as much as the near-permanent arousal of her body.

Taz released her tight hold on the persistently squeaking Graham and held him by one leg. Jude's mocking look suggested that he'd worked out the link between Graham's outbursts and her tension. The last thing she wanted was for Jude to imagine that his seduction technique was working on her—or that their past affair meant anything to her.

Time to bow out, she thought nervously, before he realised she was fatally aroused. That was the trouble with being on a sex starvation diet. Along came a master of allure and *wham*! She faked a huge yawn.

'Hey-ho! That's my cue. Riveting though this is, I'll go up now, Jude. Goodnight—'

He quickly stepped in front of her and barred the way, forcing her to stop suddenly to prevent herself from cannoning into him.

'You can't leave. Not yet!' he said firmly.

Taz's overactive mind came up with a scene immediately. He'd left Belinda sprawled across rumpled bed sheets, too sated by sex to move.

'Why?' She glared, hoping his answer wouldn't be too graphic.

'She...needs a little time to herself,' he replied, thin-lipped and evasive. Two faint spots of colour had appeared on his cheekbones and Taz was astonished to see that he was embarrassed.

Her stomach plummeted downwards. She'd been right—and apparently she couldn't deal with the thought of Jude and Belinda making love. Jerkily she said, 'It's late. I'm ready to crawl into bed...'

Going pink herself, she broke off, wishing she hadn't said the 'bed' word. Sexuality seemed to hover thickly in the air between them, and Jude's breathing had become as laboured as hers, his eyes hooded and drowsy with desire as if the combined thoughts of bed and sex had stirred his senses.

He came closer. She stopped breathing as he raised his arms, tingles of expectation sensitising the entire surface of her skin. Her eyes grew huge as his hands came around the back of her neck and she swallowed instinctively, dreading what he might do next.

CHAPTER THREE

'YOUR bow's undone,' he murmured softly.

'Uh?'

She'd meant to say a banal 'Gosh, has it?' since she'd failed to think of a sophisticated retort. But her larynx was paralysed now as well. Jude solemnly re-tied the bow, having some difficulty with its slippery silkiness.

'There,' he breathed, looking down on her stunned face.

'Uh-huh.' Taz despaired. Uh-huh! Where was biting wit when you wanted it?

When Jude didn't step back, she felt quite numbed by his nearness, her mind an utter blank. For a suspended second or two, he stared with open hunger at her parted lips as though on the brink of ravishing them.

Taz unwittingly craned her neck forward, inviting that dangerous, desperately desired kiss. And a reflex movement of her tongue had it darting out to moisten her mouth before she realised what a terminally stupid thing she was doing.

Jude exhaled harshly. 'If you want to go to bed,' he said thickly, his eyes fixed on her parted lips, 'you'll have to wait.'

I want to go to bed with you now, she thought crazily, unable to comprehend the powerful urges which were uncoiling in her long-untouched body. And her eyes opened wide with shock at her utter shamelessness, and she turned bright red with mortification.

He continued to watch her with a dark and brooding expression. She knew that look of his and she knew what was happening to her. She had a monumental desire to kiss him till he couldn't breathe, a longing deep inside her for his arms to hold her, his voice to whisper wonderful lies in her ears... *Lies*...

Taz's brain kicked back into operation before she could do anything so outrageous. 'I don't think I'll wait,' she said in panic, setting off for the lift. 'I'm going up to—'

'You're not!'

Quite summarily he grabbed her arm and spun her around. If it hadn't been for his hands holding her securely, she believed she would have fallen off her stilts and twisted both ankles.

'What the devil are you *doing*?' she demanded, scared of remaining within even ten yards of him.

'Don't go!' he ordered gruffly.

'Why...not?' she said huskily.

'Don't...be difficult, Taz,' he murmured, his mouth unnervingly moist. His hands moved up her arms, gliding with such tantalising delicacy that her whole mind became focussed on the progress of each trailing finger as it brushed her sensitive flesh. 'Do I have to make it any plainer? I don't want you to go.'

He stepped even nearer and Taz felt her opposition waning dangerously.

'Oh!' was all she could muster.

'Let's talk,' he said softly. 'The two of us.' He produced a golden smile that would have melted the hardest heart. 'And Graham, too, providing he doesn't interrupt,' he added, pitch-black eyes bright with a heart-wrenching humour.

Somewhere in the background a waiter dropped a metal tray, the noise breaking sharply into her clouded brain. Taz was jolted back into reality. This helpless hunger was terrible, terrible.

She loathed Jude for making a pass. She was disgusted with herself for being mesmerised by him even for a second. Her head cleared of its fog and she fixed him with a hard stare.

'Let me go, Jude. I'm too tired to be sociable.'

There was a flicker of annoyance and then alarm in his expression at her continued defiance. 'I'm not asking for inane cocktail party chatter from you. If you want, you can sit in total silence. All I want is that you stay here for a while,' he insisted, maintaining his grip of iron.

'Give me a reason,' she muttered, suspicious of his motives. 'I don't want to be standing here in a fake jungle with tape recordings of parrots squawking and monkeys screaming. I want to be upstairs, sipping hot cocoa and chatting to Bel while I put my curlers in and slip—'

'Into your nightdress.'

Her jaws clamped together like a vice. Curse him! That was exactly what she'd intended to say and it would have been a mistake. You didn't talk about anything intimate with Jude around. She thought of the sleek scraps of nonsense she'd bought with her credit card and decided to play safe without actually lying.

'Winceyette pyjamas. With stripes.'

'Don't believe you.'

'Grey and maroon,' she invented wildly, 'with a little monogram on the pocket—'

'Nonsense. Ivory silk, I think,' he mused, ignoring her remark. 'Something smooth and simple but beautifully cut—'

'You're playing for time,' she accused, horribly disconcerted. The description was spot-on accurate.

'Yes.'

Her mouth opened and closed at this frank admission. She turned it into another yawn. 'Well, this is jolly. Are we going to progress to *your* nightly routine now, via your teeth-flossing technique, or will you tell me why you're so darned determined to keep me down here?' she asked crossly. 'I hardly imagine it's because you long to be my best pal. And you certainly can't want to chat me up. You're an engaged man, aren't you?'

He gazed at her enigmatically from under lowered brows and didn't comment.

Unsettled, she plunged on. 'You'd better come up with something important enough to deny me my cocoa.'

His eyebrows soared up to vividly express his disbelief. 'You never drank cocoa when I knew you.'

'A girl can change her mind about a lot of things,' she said meaningfully. 'So tell me, Jude, or I'm going to start drawing attention to the fact that you're harassing me. I'm quite good at screaming, you know.'

He muttered something under his breath. 'OK. It was worth a try. Have it your way. We had an argument.'

Oh, hooray! she thought maliciously. Then, almost immediately, she felt worried about Belinda's emotional state and changed her mind.

'Nothing serious, was it?' she asked anxiously.

The dark eyes lowered, then met hers again with the full force of their black and impenetrable depths. 'Perhaps a little more physical than I'd have liked,' he admitted reluctantly.

'A *fight*? Have you been slapping her around?' Taz asked in horror.

'Don't be insulting!' he exclaimed, and he was so shocked, so angry at her rather wild accusation that she believed him. 'We had a disagreement and I had to restrain her. *Gently.* She became upset.'

'How upset?'

'Tears. I tried to calm her down, but it would be kind to give her a little more time on her own. Come and have a coffee. I want to get something straight.'

Taz bristled at his brisk and matter-of-fact attitude. Just a moment ago he was all husky and seductive. It looked to her as if his searing sex appeal had been turned on and off like a tap! Apparently he'd cranked up the charm purely because he'd wanted her to keep away from Bel, hoping he could conceal the fact that they'd quarrelled!

She felt deeply offended. And she'd been congratulating

herself that Jude had been overwhelmed by her gorgeous new look! What a fool she was! He'd been so plausible that she'd been convinced he was attracted to her. But she wouldn't be melted and then moulded into a suitably quivering jelly for his purposes!

Seething with indignation and injured pride, she began to pick off his restraining fingers, one by one. After a moment he got the message and released her, pushing his hands into his pockets and gazing at her intently. The material strained across his pelvis. Taz felt her heart bump in her chest and averted her gaze, dismayed that she found the raw carnality of his body such a turn-on.

'If Belinda's been crying,' she said as icily as possible under the circumstances, 'someone should be with her. Since you're chickening out, then I'm going up—'

'Believe me,' he muttered, 'you wouldn't want to see her as she is now, and she certainly wouldn't want to see you.'

'Nonsense!'

He threaded shaking fingers through his hair. She was fascinated by the tightening of his skin over the bones of his face. Something serious was troubling him. Not his conscience—he didn't have one. What could it be?

'Ring her.' Curtly he offered his mobile. 'Tell her you've stopped off for a drink here but will be with her soon.'

'That's a bit far-fetched. Wouldn't I opt for a free drink with her?'

'She won't care what excuse you make, only that you'll be delayed. I bet you five hundred pesetas she won't ask you to hurry up.'

'You want me to lie, then.'

His eyes were chilling. 'Only a white lie, for Belinda's sake. To allow her to salvage her pride. I think she'll suggest you take your time—in which case you can have a drink and it won't be a lie at all.'

Taz stared at him in concern. He seemed very certain. She hoicked Graham under her arm and took the phone.

'Press one,' he directed abruptly.

It was natural that his fiancée's number should have been programmed into the phone, but for some reason that upset Taz. Absently she nuzzled the giraffe's nose as she jabbed her finger on the button and put the mobile to her ear. It rang for a long time.

'What?' came Belinda's muffled voice eventually.

'Hi, it's me, Taz!' She bit her lip on hearing what sounded like a sob. Her eyes flicked up to Jude, but he'd turned away. Mystified by his rigid shoulders and tense body, she tried to speak as naturally as possible without actually lying. 'I—I'll be up in a minute. Just chatting to someone I know. Such a lively bar—'

'Don't rush,' Belinda mumbled. 'I could d-do with half an hour thish end. Place is a tip.'

Taz's heart lurched with tender sympathy. As if Bel ever did any housework—especially at midnight! Jude must have hurt her dreadfully. Beast.

'Half an hour... If you're sure it's OK...' she began gently.

'Yeah, shweetie. Byeee.'

Taz frowned as the call was abruptly disconnected. Belinda had sounded slurred, as if she'd been woken from sleep. Perhaps they'd had too many late nights and she'd dozed off for a moment.

Jude swung around on his heel, his expression unreadable. 'How did she sound?'

Oh, definitely a guilt complex there, Taz thought sourly. 'As if she'd downed a bottle of Scotch,' she exaggerated.

His mouth tightened. 'We...had a few drinks,' he muttered shiftily.

'Oh, great. You got each other tipsy and started bickering!' She flinched at his slicing glance.

'I'm not the bickering sort!' he declared, grim and annoyed. 'Stop trying to wind me up!'

'Well, it's very inconvenient. I arrive here and find I have to hang around killing time, all because you picked tonight of all nights to get sozzled and have a row!'

'You can't time arguments. They happen.'

Taz glowered. Jude would probably stand on guard in case she sloped up to the apartment three seconds before the half-hour was up. The prospect made her feel very edgy.

She opened her bag and worked her way through the jumble of essential things she always carried with her till she found her wallet and whipped out the money she owed him.

'Here you are. Five hundred pesetas.'

Jude studied her with a cynical expression. 'I'm glad you appreciate that debts should always be paid,' he said caustically, taking the notes.

'Providing they're legit,' she parried with surreal charm, knowing exactly what he was referring to: the supposed 'debt' owed to his family.

She stalked haughtily towards the in-house tapas and coffee bar, all the while mulling over his views on 'debts'. He truly believed that he and his father had been cheated out of the hospital. Unable to make headway with his revenge when her father was alive, Jude had switched his vengeance to an easier target: Belinda.

If part of his revenge took the form of playing with Bel's affections, muttering sweet nothings one minute and losing his temper the next, Taz decided she'd personally make him regret he'd ever set eyes on the Laker women.

He must know that her emotional stepmother would never survive such treatment. Taz felt a cold fear slip down her spine.

Jude's indifference and infidelity would almost certainly become apparent sooner or later. That could seriously unsettle the unstable Bel.

Upset, she paused, swaying on unsteady legs, aware that she was on the brink of despairing tears. Perhaps she was breaking her heart for Bel, perhaps for the love she'd once freely given to this cold-hearted, inhuman devil.

There was no time to lose. Her entire body shook. She had to act fast, she thought miserably, before he did untold damage.

Seeing her falter, he felt an overwhelming urge to grab her fiercely and rain hot kisses on her face and throat to prove to her that she wasn't as clever as she imagined. All her witty backchat couldn't conceal the fact that she was as confused as he was about the all-consuming sexual atmosphere between them. It was suffocating him, overriding everything else in his mind, and he knew that he wouldn't be sane again until she was naked and in his arms, sated from passion.

He hated her and he wanted her like hell. Every word from that softly parted mouth had his guts twisting with desire even though he knew that touching her would be like igniting petrol: she'd burn him, leave him disgusted with his lust and he'd end up loathing himself for letting his body rule his brain.

It had been unfortunate that he'd needed to keep Taz hanging around so that Bel had time to re-apply her make-up and hide the fact that she'd been crying. He'd given Bel a hug, had told her to put on something expensive and stunning and had promised he'd delay Taz for twenty minutes.

That time had been fatal to his self-control. On several occasions he'd been close to responding to her flirting and that annoyed him. *He* wanted to be the one who called the shots. Perhaps he would. She needed putting in her place.

Deceptively vulnerable, she stood there with her head bowed as she struggled with her volatile emotions and all he could think of was the smoothness of her exposed neck and how sweet it would taste. He was shaking, almost breathless with an unstoppable hunger.

Wrestling with it, he began to wonder if he could feel like this and meet Taz every day—and yet be married to Belinda. The answer didn't bear thinking about.

Seeing her had knocked him for six. She had become

more beautiful than he had ever imagined in his wildest dreams. And there'd been plenty of those. Touching her had driven home the devastating reality: he desired her with a desperation that drove all sense and duty and caution from his head. She was funny and beautiful, achingly sexy and far too alluring for any man's peace of mind.

His fists clenched. He was trapped in a prison of his own making. He couldn't do the honourable thing and break off his engagement. Not only might it tip the increasingly emotional Belinda over the edge, but also it could literally hasten his father's death.

Pain slashed his eyes at the cruel irony of the situation. For years he had worked for this moment, biding his time and building up his capital, investing aggressively and thinking of nothing else except a hostile takeover bid.

Laker's death had brought with it a startling opportunity: a short cut to owning the hospital which left his wealth intact. And now that justice was within his grasp Taz had to come along and wreck his plans.

A rage filled his chest to bursting. *Why* did he want her so badly? She'd proved to be as corrupt as her father. She'd lied about loving him and he knew she was bad news—yet she was like a drug. One glance from those promise-laden eyes and he was hopelessly addicted.

He fought for self-control. Inwardly he groaned, his stomach muscles contracting. He knew where his duty lay and it wasn't with his personal gratification. It was with the fragile, needy Belinda who'd clung to him like a drowning woman to a log, and with his beloved and much suffering father.

Honour weighed heavily on his shoulders. He couldn't destroy two people for a few hours of pleasure. So the beautiful Taz was taboo.

His eyes blazed with a black hatred. Somehow he had to get her out of his system—but how?

Fatally, she gave a betraying sniff. It was his cue, an excuse to touch her. He put his hands possessively on her shoulders and drew her against him. As if unaware of what she was doing, she leaned back against his chest, accepting the comfort he offered.

'Taz,' he whispered hoarsely, his mouth tantalisingly close to her soft cheek. 'Tell me what's wrong.'

Temporarily too weak to break away, Taz remained rigid with dismay, every inch of her shoulders, back and pelvis seemingly desperate to melt into Jude's tempting embrace.

But this was Bel's lover. Longing to stay, to be held by him, Taz wrenched free, grabbed at a mimosa tree and hung on for dear life, trying frantically to come up with an excuse for her lack of co-ordination.

'Gosh! Touch of giddiness,' she explained truthfully. 'Too much champagne at my farewell party, too little food. And heaven knows what they put in the punch to make it live up to its name.'

Jude didn't speak for a moment. Tense and strained, he studied her critically and, although he didn't move, she had the impression he was drawing back from her. Taz stared back, anxiously hoping he'd accepted her explanation, her eyes huge and her lips parted as her breath filtered thinly from her lungs.

Impassively he drawled, 'You'd better eat something, then, before you snap that tree in half and devour it, roots and all.'

Taz risked letting go. She felt so sick that she knew she couldn't manage a morsel. 'Caffeine and sugar will do the trick,' she muttered.

'Easier on the digestion, too,' he agreed mockingly.

She glared, launching herself perilously in the direction of the coffee shop.

Her heels rammed furiously into the terracotta tiles, her tall body jarring with each step as she tried to keep on an even keel. Apart from the occasional lurch—which meant that Jude took those opportunities to manhandle her body back to an upright position—she managed quite well.

'You seem upset or flustered about something,' he commented drily.

'Whatever gave you that idea?' She frowned, concentrating hard on the entrance ahead. 'I told you. I'm tired and hungry.'

Jude just shrugged. His perception set her teeth on edge. It was his fault she wasn't tucked up in bed right now with Graham, his fault that her mind was flooded with lovely memories so that she was almost choking with desire for a worthless rat.

She struggled to clear her head and assess the situation. Perhaps this row was not a disaster for Bel's emotions, but a godsend. Taz thought she might be able to build on the fact that the relationship had flaws in it, and persuade Bel that Jude wasn't her type. First she must find out why they'd quarrelled.

Jude caught Taz's elbow, escorting her through the glass doors and into the noisy bar. The resulting tingles that irradiated her body knocked her hopes on the head. Bel would be putty in this man's hands. The chances were, thought Taz gloomily, that her stepmother was desperate to be snuggling up to him again.

She winced. Jude's fingers tightened and she had to force herself to walk normally and not trip over her feet.

Heads were turning as they walked through the packed tables of the crowded bar. People were obviously whispering about them. Taz had a sense of *déjà vu*. She remembered when he'd been a younger man how a room had buzzed with muttered asides when he'd entered because of his extraordinary charisma.

Now, in addition to being drop-dead gorgeous, he had an enviable aura of confidence and self-assurance that drew eyes like... Her eyes flashed in scorn. Like flies to jam. Maggots to rotting meat. Snails to vegetation. She felt better and flung smiles everywhere.

As she did so, it became clear that Jude was a real babe

magnet. Hair was being patted, skirts smoothed, backs straightened, cleavages deepened. One woman even rose and brushed past Jude, clumsily—huh!—knocking into him with her pointy breasts and barring their way.

Taz seethed.

'*Perdone*,' the woman purred, her baby blues wide and innocent, though she didn't look at all sorry to Taz.

Jude appraised the voluptuous figure in the skimpy designer shift with a quick but thorough skill born of long practice.

'*No importa*,' he said graciously, receiving a flash of bleached teeth as a reward.

Just the sort of behaviour a committed, engaged man indulged in! Taz thought sarcastically. She wanted to stomp off but Jude wasn't going anywhere and his hand was cupped so firmly around her elbow that she couldn't move without dislocating her arm. So she was forced to watch while the blonde blatantly stuffed a fancy plastic visiting card down Jude's shirt-front and said huskily that she'd like him to call her.

'You can call him engaged,' she snapped in Spanish.

The woman raised an eyebrow. 'So?'

Taz bridled. 'So he's not for hire or rent. And he's allergic to cheap plastic. Comes out in spots.'

Jude grinned then sucked in his breath when Taz's hands grabbed at his stomach. Tight-lipped, she located the card through his shirt and worked it up the front of his body.

'Engaged men don't encourage liaisons with other women,' she muttered in icy reproof.

'Depends on the woman,' he said throatily.

'So I see.'

With cold contempt she extricated the vulgar piece of gold plastic with finger and thumb, holding it as if it were covered in sewage.

'Now what are you going to do with it?' he wondered.

'Don't tempt me,' she replied sourly, and handed it back to Blondie, who gave a shrug and flounced off.

'We must do this again,' he said with an amused smile. But when he teasingly smoothed his hand over his body where her hand had trawled for the card his expression told her that he'd found the experience highly arousing.

Taz firmed her mouth. 'Not this side of the next millennium!'

'I'm touched you should defend your stepmother's right to my body,' he drawled.

She blinked. That wasn't why she'd been so affronted. She'd been jealous. Appalled, she wanted to wound him.

'One of us had to. You weren't putting up much resistance to that woman. And I thought Spanish men held marriage in high regard!'

Jude glared. 'We do—'

'Could have fooled me.'

Pleased with the tensing of his body at that comment on his honour, Taz was about to move on when she felt a hand on her bottom. It wasn't Jude's—she knew how that would feel. This one was hot and fleshy. Looking down at a nearby table from her aristocratic height, she saw a merry pair of eyes twinkling at her.

'You are absolutely stunning,' their dishy English owner said appreciatively, raising a glass of Rioja to her.

'Oh, thanks!' she fluttered, where normally she would have said something sharp and crushing and whisked on.

Jude did the whisking for her. She found herself being propelled forwards so rapidly that she could hardly get her feet into synch.

'I was making a conquest there!' she protested, when the glint-eyed Jude let her go and pulled out a chair for her at a discreet table in a corner.

'I'm not hanging around like a lemon while you respond to every man here who's attracted to you,' he said frostily.

'The words "pot", "kettle" and "black" spring to

mind,' she countered, refusing the chair—which had its back to the room—out of principle and planting herself in the one opposite. 'Besides, chatting to my admirers wouldn't exactly take long!' she added with total self-honesty.

'You can't be that blind. It's obvious that all the men in this room are fantasising about getting you into bed!' he retorted cynically.

'*Are* they?' Taz exclaimed, wide-eyed in astonishment. But it seemed he could be right. Most of the men crowding around the bar were giving her the glad eye.

Whereas Jude gave her an impassive stare. 'Can't you see the way they're eating you up?'

'Perhaps the service here is bad and they're hungry,' she quipped, wondering if this was his usual line of flattery. If so, it worked. She felt gorgeous. She beamed at all and sundry just to annoy him.

'They're hungry all right. Don't do that!'

'Do what?'

'Encourage them. You should know that men here only need a flicker of an eyelash and they're all over you.'

'Mmm, I do,' she said absently.

His mouth pinched in with disapproval. He took Graham from her and irascibly stuffed the animal in a spare seat then sat in the chair she'd rejected.

'I know you've been around and you're not remotely innocent, but watch yourself with the men in this town,' he ordered abruptly, like a father lecturing a child. 'Most of them are predatory and are on the look-out for women with a healthy bank balance, and by the look of you you fit that bill.'

'Really?' she asked coolly, astounded by his gall. 'Well, for your information, I despise people like that. It turns my stomach to think of a man flattering a woman and pretending to adore her for an underhand reason.' She met his gaze in challenge. 'I think it's disgusting and squalid, don't you?'

His brows zapped together but he could hardly disagree. 'Yes,' he clipped. 'I do.'

'A man like that,' she went on ruthlessly, 'is virtually selling his body in exchange for something he wants! That means he's no better than a male prostitute!'

If she'd hit a raw nerve, he didn't show it by even a flicker of his facial muscles. For a few seconds he met her gaze without blinking but his eyes slowly narrowed to dark slits.

'Deception of any kind is wrong,' he agreed softly, 'and deserves to be punished.'

Her courage failed her for a moment. He seemed to be addressing his remark specifically to her. Perhaps Jude knew that she would do almost anything to stop his forthcoming wedding! Her hands trembled. But she'd chosen her course and had to pursue it to the bitter end.

'You're so right!' she agreed grimly. 'If any snake-hipped gigolo tries it on with Bel or me, I'll make his life hell!'

Jude's eyes mocked her. 'I'll make sure word gets about. As a matter of interest, what would you do, Taz?' he enquired.

'Something utterly low-down and sneaky which would hit him where his pride sits,' she replied darkly.

'Ah. A man's pride. You must mean somewhere below the belt?'

She met his amused eyes and felt the anger stir within her. She'd give him amused! 'Absolutely. I hope you're marrying Bel for love,' she ventured recklessly.

He merely stared, his eyes hooded and secretive.

Taz tried another tack. Her fingers idly traced the appliqué leaves on the tablecloth. 'Shame about the tiff. What was your row about?'

'Personal.' His abruptly shuttered face defied her to persist with the subject. 'Taz, what's done is done. The row and its causes are between the two of us. Keep out of it and let me handle it my way...*café solo y coñac*,' he said, breaking off with finality and addressing the hovering waiter. 'Taz?'

'*Café con leche, coñac, por favor.*' She frowned. 'Jude, it's not my business what happened between you both, but...I feel uncomfortable sitting here while she's upset and all on her own. I care about Bel—'

'That's not the point. She doesn't want you around, does she?' he argued. His eyes were cynical. 'We have to respect her space.'

Taz flung him a scathing look. That kind of remark sat uneasily with Jude's macho and politically incorrect outlook. He'd made it clear that there were two kinds of women: those for bed and fun, and those for marriage and the kitchen.

'I know that, but—'

'Then let her calm down in private. Trust me on this.'

To coax her, he was relying on his charisma again. He had fixed her with his disconcerting glowing gaze, his voice low and intimate. Even though she knew this fact, she came close to falling under his spell. Taz had to work hard to snap out of the lovely sensation that she was turning into a warm and viscous liquid where she sat.

Trust him? She'd rather trust a flesh-deprived piranha and attach it to her thigh.

'You're so amazingly persuasive,' she said with total truth.

Jude wasn't able to hide his relief. A complacent smile lit his face. 'I'm glad you're being sensible and sensitive to Bel's needs,' he flattered smoothly. 'As a matter of fact I'm glad we can have a few extra moments on our own. It gives us an opportunity to get one or two things clear.'

'Like what?' she asked, immediately wary of his glib patter.

'To start with...can I have your promise that we're agreed Belinda shouldn't be told we know each other from way back?'

I *don't* know you, Taz mused with inner sorrow. You are a stranger.

She kept him waiting for her answer, stirring her coffee as if in deep contemplation. He was afraid she'd condemn him. It was her plan that he'd condemn himself, but she wasn't going to tell him that.

'I'm not sure.' Solemnly she met his tense gaze. 'Shouldn't we be honest with her?'

Jude's lips compressed and then were forced back into the semblance of a thin smile. 'Is that wise? As you said, it was just a teenage thing. Why trouble her by mentioning it? We wouldn't be lying, just—'

'Economical with the truth.' She stared at the froth in her cup as if it held the answers to the universe in it.

Jude shifted irritably in his chair. 'It would upset her.'

'She can hardly think you're a virgin,' Taz said caustically. 'Anyone can see you've got plenty of experience under your belt and all points north.'

The smile was cancelled. 'I mean,' he said through his teeth, 'that she'd feel awkward knowing I'd dated you as well.'

Dated and bedded. Taz felt a twinge of discomfort. It was a bizarre situation and she knew it would probably devastate the insecure Bel. 'But if she found out later—' she demurred, twisting the knife.

'How could she? Only three people know of our past relationship. You, me, and my father.' There was a tense pause. Jude's face darkened. 'Father...' He clamped his lips together as if holding something back then started again, his voice gravelly. 'Father won't say anything. And I never will. However, if you want to hurt Belinda, go ahead, tell her.'

Of course she had to protect Bel. But it bothered her that she couldn't be entirely up front with her stepmother. Still, keeping silent on the matter didn't constitute a lie and it would be for the best.

'I suppose you're right,' she said slowly. 'Bel would want to know all the gory details and that would be a disaster for you, wouldn't it?'

'What do you mean?' he asked guardedly.

'I'd have to explain how we parted,' she said flatly. 'It would reflect badly on you.' Jude flushed beneath his tan as if embarrassed at the reminder of his caddish behaviour. 'You lied about loving me so that you could get me into bed and coax information out of me about the hospital. Bel might wonder if you made a habit of being devious, mightn't she?'

There was an icy pause. 'To the untrained ear, that could sound almost as if you're threatening me,' he said coldly.

'Why would I do that?' she countered.

'Revenge. Because...you think I tricked you into losing your virginity,' he said in a low voice.

She winced, quickly replacing the cup and isolating her hands on her lap before any coffee was spilled.

'Revenge is vile, Jude,' she answered, her face pale.

'And justice?' he enquired softly.

'That's different. I'm a firm believer in it.'

They stared at one another for a moment or two, their black brows angled in frowns, pained eyes reflecting one another's dark memories.

'So am I,' he said heavily. 'May God help me.'

And then Taz knew from the fierce conviction in his voice that he would stop at nothing to achieve his goal. All her talk of purple satin and fractious children had been in vain. Jude's mind was made up.

Her hands closed around her cup. She was fighting a cultural trait that had its roots in history. Andalusians were an intensely passionate people, known for their feuds and bitter resentments that were never forgotten—and which sometimes had continued through the centuries.

Families stuck together against outsiders and even neighbours, and family honour was to be protected at all costs. Andalusian honour took priority over personal wishes.

Jude could never rest till he'd ruined his father's enemy— or *any* member of the Laker family.

Jude stubbornly believed his father had substantially invested in the hospital and that Corderro involvement had persuaded the bank to loan the remaining sum necessary. For years Jude had harboured a grudge that had no justification.

The result was that two people were to be married—and one of them would quickly find that her dreams had turned to ashes.

'Jude,' she said shakily, appalled by what he intended, 'all I want is for Belinda to be happy and secure—'

'She is. I will look after her. And because of that we say nothing of the links between you and me.'

Her eyes filled with anguish at her helplessness to change Jude's beliefs. It would be war, then. She'd have to persuade Belinda to dump him.

But, because of Bel's fragile personality, she couldn't reveal that he was marrying her for revenge, and she couldn't say that he didn't give a damn about her. Gloomily she picked up her coffee spoon and aimlessly stirred away. How on earth was she going to split them up? She sighed and realised Jude was tensely waiting for confirmation from her.

'The past is over and done with. We should look to the future,' she fudged eventually.

'I agree. Though…' His forefinger idly stroked the satiny petals of the roses on the table. 'There are moments in the past,' he said quietly, 'that I'll never forget.'

'Me too,' she croaked.

Pained, she lowered her eyes.

Shortly after Mateo's preposterous claim that he'd invested heavily in the hospital and should have some say in its development, Jude had come to see her.

They'd quarrelled. He'd tried to make her agree that his father was in the right. But she'd heard the true story from her own father, and knew Jude's part in the scam.

Bitter at being used as a means of commercial gain, she'd refused to listen to his ridiculous accusation that her father had conned the Corderros out of a fortune and had said so, in no uncertain terms.

'Then it's over between us, Taz,' he'd said with quiet finality.

'Because I won't believe your lies?' she'd asked in astonishment.

'Because this isn't Romeo and Juliet!' he'd snapped. 'I cannot, in all conscience, consort with the daughter of the man who seems determined to fleece my father!'

'And what of your undying love for me?' she'd queried, so numb that there hadn't been even a shake in her voice.

He'd shrugged, avoiding her eyes. 'Did you believe in that?' he'd asked harshly.

Her stomach had contracted with the shock and it was anger that had kept her from revealing the depths of her misery. 'My father said it was a sham. I wonder what you were thinking when we looked at those wedding magazines and we were planning our family and the house we'd live in?' she'd said bitterly.

Then his head had lifted, all the arrogance and pride of a Spanish male in the curl of his lip and the flare of his nostrils. 'Taz, there's one thing you must understand. We Corderros only marry people of breeding.'

As rejections went, it had been a stunner and she'd realised her mistake in surrendering her virginity to a plausible, passionate Spaniard.

It had been her pride that had saved her from howling her eyes out there and then. With her adrenaline running high and protecting her, she'd surveyed him coolly.

'What a snob you are, Jude. And yet you're the son of a con man and have inherited his lack of morals, it seems.'

He hadn't seemed to register her insult. 'And you, Taz,' he'd said quietly. 'Did you...love me?'

It was a while before she'd found the right answer. 'Do I look devastated because our relationship has broken up?' she'd asked with scorn.

'No. You don't,' he'd said heavily. There was a long and tense silence before he'd muttered, 'Goodbye, Taz.'

And he'd gone.

That was when she'd broken down. With him had gone all her dreams. And although she'd known she'd been well and truly conned her heart hadn't been ready to accept that truth. So she'd turned to food for comfort.

Taz morosely dragged herself back to the present. Never again would she put her trust in Jude, she vowed. Even if every fibre of her being still responded to him.

CHAPTER FOUR

IN THE tapas bar, Taz bit her lip to hold back a moan, the noise of people's chatter making her head pound. Reliving those memories had weakened her. Briefly she was back in that unloved, plump body, her confidence at rock-bottom.

'Are you thinking of us?' Jude asked darkly. 'If so—'

'*No!*' she choked. And she wanted to make him feel bad. 'My father!' she hurled at him with a sob.

'I see,' he said, instantly stiff and remote. 'I'm surprised. I didn't know you'd loved him at all. You'd told me you hardly knew him.' He grunted. 'Blood will out, though, won't it? You chose to believe him, not me.'

She searched for her handkerchief and blew her nose. There had been little love in her life. Her father had been too busy wheeler-dealing, socialising and womanising to have much time for his daughter—especially the abandoned child of a second wife who'd run away with the chauffeur. Taz had been left in no doubt as to her mother's promiscuous, ungrateful nature.

As soon as possible, Taz had been shipped off to England to be educated. She'd stayed with a host family and had occasionally returned to spend the holiday periods in Spain, when she'd been left to her own devices.

Oddly, Jude's betrayal had brought her closer to her father. They'd spent long hours together discussing the situation, and she had learned the whole sordid story from start to finish.

Jude had ruthlessly courted her in order to find out what he could about the hospital project. She remembered showing Jude the plans and eagerly answering his probing questions. She'd been duped, there was no doubt about that, and her father's subsequent affection had been the one recompense for the misery she'd endured at Jude's hands.

Once more Taz felt the pain of his vicious rejection, the loneliness, and the desperation that had brought her to the depths of self-loathing. For a painful few moments she lived all over again the sensation of being desperately unhappy, betrayed and abandoned.

Tears started in her eyes. Clutching the brandy glass with great care, she tossed the drink down in one gulp before she blearily met his intense gaze.

'Cognac makes my eyes water!' she mumbled.

'That's not why you're upset,' he said tightly. 'You clearly loved him very much.'

She thought of Jude and fiddled miserably with her coffee spoon. 'Oh, I loved him!'

He sighed heavily. 'Much as I deplore your judgement, I do understand. I know how strong the bond can be between father and child. It ties them together and keeps them bound for the rest of their lives. Taz...you're bending that.'

Jude rescued the mangled teaspoon, his fingers brushing hers. She felt a kick of desire in the pit of her stomach as every part of her body responded to his unexpected touch.

Her startled eyes met his and she knew he had felt the same lightning bolt of pure need. For a brief second his hand enveloped hers tightly and she half closed her eyes at the pleasure that gave her.

Appalled, she crossly pushed the spoon away, knocking over the sugar bowl and the menu card as she did so.

Jude retrieved both. 'We shouldn't be at each other's throats like this. There's too much between us. I want us to be friends and I think you want that too.' And he turned his soft brown eyes on her, their fierce message plain for her to see.

She hated him then. There was no doubt about Jude's intention. For 'friends', substitute 'lovers'. Blatant sensuality flowed from every pore in a direct male challenge: Here I am, let's have some fun, to hell with fidelity. Her mouth was dry, her heartbeat seemingly leaping in her throat. Jude was utterly irresistible and totally without conscience.

She couldn't believe that he was able to sit opposite her and make overtures while his future wife drifted miserably around the penthouse suite a short distance away, smarting from their recent spat. Suddenly she wanted to leave, sickened by his greed for sexual gratification.

White-faced, she rose from her seat. 'I really must go—'

'Just a moment,' he ordered. 'There's something else we must discuss.'

Ice-cold, she gazed down at him. 'Let me guess,' she said scathingly. 'You don't want Belinda to know that my father and yours were in a dispute over the ownership of the David Laker Hospital.'

Jude nodded slowly, his eyes hard as they assessed her mood. 'She's…emotional at the moment. So much has happened to her in a short time: David's death…inheriting his fortune…meeting me… She needs someone to help manage her financial affairs and run the hospital properly. What she *doesn't* need is aggravation. Little things can easily upset her—'

'Jude,' she said coldly, 'I know Bel better than you do and I wouldn't do *anything* to hurt her. But I do want to be of some help. And I can't in all conscience stay down here chatting to you any longer.'

Plainly annoyed, he shrugged and admitted defeat. 'In that case,' he said tautly, 'I'd better come up with you.'

She could hardly stop him. In strained silence they took the lift to the penthouse suite. Jude was extremely tense, his fists clenching and unclenching by his sides, and the angle of his jaw was rock-hard.

Taz felt a bitter pleasure at his discomfort. She rang the bell but he was already slipping a key into the lock and she felt her stomach churn at his action. It was difficult, she thought ruefully, dealing with this intimate relationship between her stepmother and her ex-lover!

Looking oddly haggard, Jude snapped on the light, his eyes darting about the lobby keenly as if afraid of seeing something unpleasant, though she couldn't understand what it might be. Taz's dark brows met in a puzzled frown as he moved into the large sitting room beyond, which was surprisingly tidy.

'Belinda?' he called edgily. 'Taz is here.'

Taz entered the room with its enormous picture windows overlooking the marina. Astounding floral displays filled the air with perfume but there was an odd, underlying sour smell she couldn't identify.

Checking an instinctive sense of unease, Taz strolled around her luggage and the assorted carrier bags that had been left in the middle of the room.

'Hi, Bel!' she called, dumping Graham and whipping off her hat. Jude stared at her hair for a moment, his eyes soft and liquid.

'I'll check the bedrooms,' he said hoarsely.

She caught up with him in what had been the guest room and she assumed that Belinda had moved into it because the wardrobe was full of Bel's clothes and two dresses were lying on the bed.

Jude looked across at her, his face set impassively. 'She's gone out.'

'Oh!' So much for her stepmother being upset. She'd taken herself out to a nightclub or something. Jude seemed surprised that Belinda could be so feisty. 'Never mind,' she said waspishly. 'I'm sure she's having fun.' Feeling deflated and oddly depressed, she returned to the sitting room and made for the sofa, where she kicked off her stilts and rubbed her aching arches. 'I'll say goodnight, then.'

Jude muttered something under his breath and punched a button on his mobile. Leaning back, Taz felt something hard in her back and rooted around beneath the cushion, bringing out an empty bottle of wine. Belinda really was scatty, she thought fondly, putting the bottle on the table next to the single glass.

Waiting—apparently in vain—for someone to answer his call, Jude seemed transfixed by the sight of the bottle, his mouth tight with disgust. Taz felt obliged to defend Bel's bizarre disposal system.

'A loving heart is better than an organised personality,' she said pointedly. 'Mind you, if she and I are to co-own the hospital, I'll have to—'

'*What* did you say?' barked Jude, abandoning his call.

Taz blinked. 'A loving heart—'

'No! The other part!' he said grimly.

For a moment she didn't understand and then the truth dawned.

Belinda had clearly omitted to tell Jude that the Laker fortune hadn't been left to her in its entirety! Taz tucked her feet up on the sofa and met his tense interest coolly, even though her heart was thumping hard.

'About co-owning the hospital?' she queried, taunting him.

His shoulders rose with his indrawn breath. 'Don't play cat and mouse. Answer the damn question!'

'I've come to live here and take my share of the inheritance. Father divided everything between the two of us,' she said in a small voice, awed by Jude's peculiar stillness.

A twitch at the corner of his mouth betrayed the effort he was making to maintain control of himself. 'You...have a half share?'

He swore under his breath and stared at her for several seconds as if shell-shocked. Then he raked in a rasping breath and with a ramrod-stiff spine he strode out to the balcony.

Taz felt sick. This was absolute and final confirmation that he'd wooed Belinda for another prize entirely. He hadn't bargained on sharing the hospital with anyone. Taz's hands shook. What would he do now?

Nervously she uncurled her long legs and stumbled to the kitchen for a glass of water. Perhaps he'd vent his spleen on her stepmother. Whatever the case, he was clearly extremely angry. Taz quailed, fearful of the consequences.

She heard him returning, his stride impatient and rapid. She smoothed her hands over her hips and turned to face him. His expression was impossible to read.

'I'm going to find Belinda,' he announced flatly.

'Jude! Wait!'

In alarm, she caught the sleeve of his shirt just when he was turning away. At her touch he froze in his tracks as though she'd stunned him with a laser gun.

'Let go of me!' he grated furiously.

She gulped, afraid of him, but hung on. 'Wait till you've calmed down. You're angry...' Her voice trailed to nothing, silenced by the deep anguish that carved his mouth into bitter lines.

'You don't know the half of it,' he said in an undertone.

'Jude, I beg you, don't be angry with her for not telling you that I had a share too,' she begged, her eyes wide and pleading as she stared into his face. His breath felt hot on her mouth but she forced herself not to respond to the curls of pleasure his nearness was producing. 'She's forgetful, not devious. I doubt it occurred to her that it might be of interest. You won't be hard on her, will you?'

He didn't speak—and perhaps he couldn't. The pain was now filling every line of his face, the agony in his eyes hurting her so much that she couldn't bear to look.

The hospital—and his father's vengeance—meant much more to him than she'd ever realised. He was horrified at the prospect of sacrificing his freedom in exchange for just a part-share. She could feel his shock coming at her in waves and it upset her unbearably.

Why do I *care*? she asked herself in despair. He didn't

deserve her concern. And yet she felt unutterably miserable.
A tear rolled down her cheek.

'Don't do that!' he ground out hoarsely.

'I—I can't help it! I'm afraid for her...' she choked out.

'You're the one who should be afraid.'

'Why?' she gasped.

'You must know. You can't be that blind.'

His thumb pushed up her chin but she kept her eyes lowered as small silvery teardrops squeezed from the corners of
her eyes. She waited tensely for some cutting remark, a con-
temptuous comment.

Instead, she felt his hand cradle the back of her head and
then the hardness of his lips as they claimed her mouth in a
ruthless, possessive kiss.

By the time she'd gathered her wits and had knuckled her
eyes clear he was halfway across the room. When she
croaked out his name he kept on going, his body a watery
blur as it disappeared behind the closing door.

She didn't know why she was crying. She couldn't fathom
why that kiss had seemed so desperate and heartfelt when
he'd only been behaving with his usual arrogance.

He wanted to dominate her physically, perhaps to drag
her under his spell again. But he wouldn't. Once bitten was
one bite too many.

Still she felt miserable, overwhelmed by a huge sense of
loss.

Why? *Why?*

Distraught, she paced up and down the apartment, going
over and over everything that had happened.

Her plan to halt Jude in his tracks had started promisingly.
At the beginning it had seemed almost like a game. Granted,
the matter was serious, but it had been fun to meet Jude's
sinister intentions with wit and subversive humour.

Now events had taken on a different tone entirely. The
old attraction between herself and Jude was simmering beneath the surface, ready to erupt at the slightest provocation.

And Jude would provoke her as often as possible because he hadn't found love and, judging by his behaviour, he was probably still consoling himself with casual sex whenever he wanted it.

The picture was becoming clearer. She touched her mouth with a questing forefinger, feeling its plush softness as she assessed Jude's attitude and his transparent unhappiness. As she'd planned, her jokey portrayal of his future with Belinda had brought him up sharp and had clearly appalled him. Yet he couldn't back down because he would be dishonouring his solemn promise to his father.

Vaguely she stared out into the bay. Lights twinkled on the shore and the luxurious yachts in the marina. People were laughing and enjoying themselves down there, while up here she was feeling as if she'd shouldered an impossible burden.

But there was a glimmer of hope. His unhappiness was the key. If he was so miserable now, maybe she could persuade him that it would be worse if he were married to a woman he didn't love—particularly if the prize was only half won. The hospital wouldn't be totally under his control after all. She must convince him that the revenge would bring him no satisfaction, only heartache.

And yet there was his stiff Spanish pride, his obligation to his father. She frowned. Mateo Corderro was the key to this somehow...

Suddenly she became fully alert. Jude's father adored him. If she could reach the man and open his eyes to the fact that his beloved son was ruining his life from a sense of duty, she might succeed in ending this stupid vendetta.

A little more hopeful now, Taz wandered to the spare bedroom and began to undress. Somehow she and Jude would come to an agreement with the intervention of Mateo Corderro. Belinda would be let down as gently as possible. There would be no marriage, no bitterness, and no long-term damage.

Thoughtfully she plumped up the pillows, only to discover Belinda's nightdress and a hanky beneath them. That was odd. Could she have made a mistake? Perhaps this was Belinda's bedroom after all!

Uncertainly, Taz looked around and realised from the personal items around that, although the full wardrobe and the discarded dresses on the bed in the adjoining bedroom had made it look as if Bel had settled herself there, it must have been purely an overspill for the rest of her clothes.

With a resigned sigh she picked up her things and moved next door. Sliding on her satin nightie, she crawled into bed, too shattered to think any longer. She had a possible solution to the problem and she should be pleased.

Instead she continued to feel an overriding sensation of sadness. To her surprise, she began to cry again. And she saw the dawn rise before she finally slept, her pillow wet with tears.

It was almost dawn by the time Jude arrived at La Quinta. The winding road into the mountains had forced him to concentrate and thus had tempered the impotent wrath that had gripped him after Taz's revelation. Tiredness was inexorably stealing over him.

Wearily he eased himself from his car, his emotions back in cold storage again.

They'd nearly lost the estate when the business world had turned against them after the investigation. Jude's whole life had been thrown into upheaval because of a pair of dark, seductive eyes and a common crook. Used to a life of luxury, privilege and respect, he'd had to leave his law studies and slave night and day to keep the land his family had owned for centuries.

Now the estate was secure. Only the matter of revenge remained.

Thinking of this, he went—as always—to the suite of rooms in the west wing of the beautiful old farmhouse and

knocked very softly on the heavy oak door, knowing that
his insomniac father would be glad to see him.

For a while, he sat in the chair by the bed talking about
the evening's events—but leaving out his row with Belinda
about her drinking. And then, without meaning to, he said,
'I have some surprising news.'

He wondered if he sounded too casual, but somehow he
had to disguise the destructive bitterness that he felt. It had
been a cruel quirk of fate that had dangled the luscious Taz
before him at a time when he was committed to someone
else. If he'd known the situation he could have taken direct
revenge and married Taz, but fate had decreed otherwise.
He cleared his throat.

'Do you remember Taz?' he asked lightly. 'She's back in
Banus and planning to stay.'

One wink. And a small tear.

'I know,' he said gently, leaning forward in concern. 'It
brings it all back. Don't worry, the little minx won't be a
problem this time. We'll get control of the hospital, I promise.'

He wondered why he hadn't explained that Taz might
have something to say about that, since she was a co-owner.
But his father didn't need to be bothered with any more
worries than the ones he already had. Jude frowned at his
feet, his mind working overtime. Perhaps he could buy Taz
out. The Lakers were a greedy lot.

He raised his eyes and saw that his father looked strained.
'You need some rest,' he said quietly. 'Let me settle you
down. I too must get a few hours in before I return to the
penthouse. I've decided to set a wedding date—some time
in the next couple of months, Father.' He forced a smile. 'A
bird in the hand, as the English say!' he joked. His heart
hurt and he knew he had to get away. 'Goodnight,' he muttered. 'Sleep well. Go with God.'

With great care he adjusted the pillows behind his father's
head, kissed the sunken cheeks and went out. When he was

sure no one would see, he allowed his features to show the distress and hopelessness that he felt.

His father was deteriorating rapidly.

For years Mateo Corderro had tenaciously clung to life, surviving despite the poor medical diagnosis. It had been a desire for justice that had kept the stubborn spirit burning in the frail body.

Heavy-hearted, Jude entered his bedroom and walked quickly to his open window, breathing in the fragrance of a rampantly climbing banksia rose.

Jude was painfully aware that he must marry Laker's widow quickly before his father died. Jude's whole being revolted against such an idea. If only Belinda could fall in love with someone! Then he could switch his attentions to Taz.

He closed his eyes, thinking inevitably of Taz, almost choking on the desire to hold her soft body against his, to kiss her till her warm lips parted.

What a hell of a situation. He wanted the detested Taz and he couldn't have her. Yet, if he had stalled on Belinda's proposal for a few weeks, things would have been so different. He grunted. Such was life.

But...he couldn't help but think that in those circumstances he could have allowed his feelings full rein. He could have made love to Taz and, in doing so, driven her into that hazy world they'd once inhabited during their passionate encounters. Then he would have persuaded her to marry him and she would have been under his control, mind and body.

He sighed in exasperation. As it was, when he was married to Belinda he must look at Taz and never touch. Torturing himself, he thought of her dark, wicked eyes and moist mouth that had so sorely tempted him, her dangerously sinuous body and luminous skin. He imagined his lips inexorably moving over those fantastic legs, travelling their length to the silky thighs...

He shook his head, trying to rid himself of his terrible addiction. He had a duty to fulfil. Honour and duty. *Dios!* How he hated those words now!

Shafts of light were permeating the sky and the strong, agonisingly pure song of the joyful dawn chorus split the air, poignantly contrasting with his own bitter, inner darkness. Another dawn, he thought grimly, one he felt barely able to face.

Carmen woke him some five hours later by slamming back the shutters and, incongruously, singing some dreadful pop song. She looked after his father now—with his help. Increasingly he was taking a larger part in those duties because Carmen was becoming slower and her arthritis was causing her problems. Soon he might have to employ a nurse for both of them.

He stumbled blearily towards the bathroom, hassled by her good-natured insistence that he dress warmly since the wind was bitter.

'It's like a summer's day already, Carmen. Time you dug out your bikini,' he muttered sourly.

She chided him as only a sixty-eight-year-old who'd changed his nappies could, and said darkly that he'd catch his death and why didn't he wear a vest like decent God-fearing people?

'I'm young and active. I don't need to be warmed up,' he snapped, and then apologised, saying he'd got out of bed the wrong side. It wasn't Carmen's fault that he would live to regret committing himself to a marriage without passion or desire.

Feeling decidedly moody and bad-tempered—and hating that negativity—he ate his breakfast on the terrace. Ironically he was treated to all the delights which had once compensated him for his loveless existence: the sound of ecstatic birdsong, a wall of fragrance billowing in great drifts towards him from his flower fields. White doves fluttered through the fountains in front of him and against the deep blue sky the snowy Sierra stood out a stark and blinding white.

Unfortunately it all reminded him of a particular occasion when he'd kissed Taz.

A fierce stab of desire shafted through his loins and he ruthlessly crushed it. He had to see Laker's widow and bring the date of the wedding forward—perhaps enchant her with the idea of a 'quickie' somewhere romantic. Only then could he feel safe from Taz's fatal fascination.

Grim-faced, and as cold and as hard as ice inside, he drove to the apartment building and let himself in. He felt sick to the stomach and it was all he could do not to turn around and walk out. But he thought of his father and forced himself to go through with his promise.

He'd not known which of the bedrooms Belinda inhabited, but his earlier search had identified it as the one overlooking the marina. Anxious not to wake Taz, he walked softly across the thick carpet and tapped lightly on the door.

When there was no answer, he opened it slightly. His breath sucked in because it was Taz lying there, not Belinda. Perhaps, he thought, they'd swapped rooms. Confused, he hesitated, unable to resist one long look before he closed the door.

She was deeply asleep. His pulses quickened. Uncovered, she lay on her side in an abandoned posture, the linen sheets crumpled around her slender feet and baring the gleaming skin of her long and slender legs. Her dark hair fanned out over the pillow and the winceyette pyjamas were nowhere in sight. There wasn't much of her nightdress in evidence either, he noticed, his throat drying.

Thin satin straps and a dipping bodice barely held her magnificent breasts that swelled in two achingly touchable, perfect globes above the pale ivory material. Her waist looked tiny, the plushness of her hip had him clenching his fists and gritting his teeth and it was all he could do not to strip off his clothes and rush forward to kiss every delectable inch of that gleaming, dark honey skin.

He drank her in, hating her. Perfect pink toenails, smooth thighs that demanded to be caressed. Lissom naked back, its arch begging for the imprint of his mouth. Long, graceful neck, strong-boned face, soft and deliciously sleepy lips...

Choking, Jude walked out and made himself a cup of strong espresso, determined to get a grip before waking Belinda and suggesting they elope. A bitter taste rose to his mouth at the thought. This was going to be harder than he'd ever imagined but he could do it—he *must*.

Leaning against the cold stainless-steel worktop, he began to tame his rampaging desire by thinking sternly of his sick father, his horticulture business, the number of La Quinta's hectares under glass, the percentage cultivated, how much was a carefully managed wildlife habitat...

'Bel?' came Taz's sleepy voice.

Jude groaned, the figures in his head making way for one that was more delectable and far more touchable.

'No! It's—'

Too late to warn her. She'd appeared in the doorway, hair tumbling over her shoulders, and she looked soft and lush and pink from sleep and utterly irresistible.

'You!' she accused, eyes wide with alarm. She crossed her hands over her breasts where her nipples were budding hard and stiff beneath the flimsy satin.

One stretch of his hand and he could touch her and feel those breasts throbbing beneath his fingers. One impassioned groan from him and she would surely be in his arms. How he stopped himself he didn't know.

'Me,' he said huskily. And he swallowed hard to break up the lump in his throat. He ached for her. Now. Ached to hold her, stroke and kiss her. He turned away and searched for some biscuits to give his body a chance to cool down.

'What happened to the winceyettes?' he drawled.

'It was hot. Wait a minute,' she croaked.

He was glad to. He stood there taking in great gulps of air, slowing his pulses and feeling the painful pressure against his chinos beginning to recede.

For safety, he dragged out one of the arty steel chairs and settled himself at the kitchen table with his coffee and a box of chocolate biscuits.

'I imagine you came to see Bel,' she said tautly, stalking into the kitchen a little while later. 'Well, she hasn't come back. I've just checked.'

Relieved she'd put on a T-shirt and shorts—even though they were too well-fitting to disguise her fabulous body—he grabbed a biscuit and munched it, digesting her information as well.

Her news excited him. They were alone, then. So tempting. The air seemed hot and thick, laden with promise.

'She's probably on my boat,' he said curtly. 'She loves it. Perhaps she left a message.'

His tension mounting, he picked up his mobile and checked the voice mail, listening to Bel's breathless tones. When her chatter ended, he tapped a key to see where she'd been phoning from. Up came a number he didn't recognise. He put in a search on his electronic database and came up with the answer: the home number of Harvey Hoskin, the hospital manager. He frowned.

'Something wrong?' asked Taz anxiously.

'No. She went to see a friend—Harvey Hoskin.'

'And that annoys you?'

Still puzzling the situation out, he erased his frown then looked up at Taz thoughtfully. He thought it best to avoid answering. 'It was rude of her not to let you know where she was.'

She filled the kettle. 'So long as she's OK. I imagine she rushed to the person she thought would comfort her best after your row.'

Jude nodded slowly. 'I suppose you're right,' he said, a suspicion forming in his mind as he remembered how well

Bel and Harvey had got on together, giggling like old friends who were totally at ease with one another.

His pulses began to race. Supposing they were more than friends? That would be his way out and he could turn his attentions to Taz. His heart began to pound and, not wanting to raise his hopes only to have them dashed, he tried to tell himself that this was wishful thinking, nothing more.

Taz was investigating the contents of the fridge. With a bowl of eggs in one hand, she banged a pan down on the cooker behind him and continued speaking.

'She and Harvey have been friends for a long time. They come from the same part of the world, I believe. Bodmin, in Cornwall. She talked a lot about their similar backgrounds and how they'd often reminisced together. Shall I give her a message when I see her?' she asked frostily, emerging into his vision again and grabbing a crock of butter.

'No. It's something I must do myself. It's…about…our future,' he said, suddenly doubting that he could go through with the marriage at all, let alone bring it forward.

Taz abruptly disappeared behind him again. 'Bridesmaids and that?' she said jerkily.

Despite his gloom he found himself smiling faintly as he remembered her preposterous suggestions. 'Not exactly.'

'She…' Taz's voice faltered. 'She loves you very much.'

'No,' he said quietly, tired of pretence and of Taz's belief that he was the evil seducer and Bel the victim. 'She doesn't love me at all.'

He heard a knife clatter to the worktop and sensed she'd stiffened. The back of his neck prickled with her nearness.

'If that's true…then why—why are you getting married?'

'Because it is convenient.'

'Jude! How could you?' she gasped.

'How could *she*?' he countered. 'She knows the score. She's perfectly aware I don't love her, and she doesn't love me. She has her reasons, I have mine—and they're no one's business but our own.'

'She does love you, Jude. Very much.' She sounded miserable.

'I assure you she doesn't.'

'How can I believe you?' she muttered.

'You can ask her, since you evidently don't trust my word.'

She was wavering, almost believing him but not quite. 'If what you say is true,' she said quietly, 'you're both doing something dreadful. I beg you, Jude, think again. Don't throw your life away...' She checked herself. 'Don't let Bel make the mistake of entering a loveless marriage.'

He winced, hating what he was doing. 'Don't judge us, Taz. You don't know the circumstances,' he said hoarsely.

She went silent but her tension surrounded him. Like a condemned man eager to enjoy his last moments on earth, he turned his chair around to enjoy the view of her lissom body as she moved about preparing her breakfast, her clumsiness and hot face a good clue to the thoughts which must be teeming through her head.

Desire kicked in at once and it was all he could do not to plant his hands on her tiny waist and pull her backwards till she was sitting on his lap. There was something appealingly vulnerable about her as she fumbled in the china dish for the eggs he'd brought from his farm the day before.

Enchantingly different from the witty and sleek sophisticate of yesterday, she seemed to be still fogged from sleep, her movements slow and careful, and her hand constantly sweeping back the heavy fall of dark chocolate hair.

Despite all his vows to wipe her from his mind, he knew he was succumbing helplessly to her. His avid eyes focussed on her throat and then the sweet angle of her jaw—the only part of her face that was visible. Every bone in his body ached for her and suddenly the need to be close to her was overwhelming.

It wouldn't hurt. Perhaps one last kiss. A final goodbye.

Condemned man's breakfast. Unless she wanted him too, in which case...

God. It was worth a try.

'Can I help?' he asked recklessly.

Her back stiffened and she looked over her shoulder in alarm. When her hand faltered, an egg flew from her fingers, falling to the worktop and cracking open.

'Oh!' she breathed.

Jude leapt up as her arm jackknifed wildly and he just managed to save the entire bowl of eggs from annihilation. A whisk and a fork clattered to the floor, however. They both bent to pick them up, their eyes meeting, millimetres away, before they slowly straightened, breathing shallowly.

A wonderful melting sensation permeated his whole body and he found that he was hardly able to breathe at all.

'You...startled me.' Oddly hoarse, Taz shakily reached for some kitchen roll.

'Let me.'

She was trembling. Excitement raged through him unchecked. He swept away the mess, took another egg and cracked it to join the others.

'Scrambled?' he asked, thinking that his own brain was definitely addled.

This was folly in the extreme but she smelt so good, was so close, that his nerves were screaming at him to take her in his arms, to do unmentionable things to her.

'Mmm.' There was a silence and then she spoke again. 'Jude...while you're here...I—I decided something last night. I want to say something important.'

He saw the convulsive movement in her throat and knew she wanted him badly. He pushed the bowl of eggs to one side and waited, his heart pounding. He wanted her to apologise for ever doubting him in the past, to look at him and issue an unmistakable invitation. Which he would accept.

Knowing that, he realised he couldn't marry Belinda. He wanted Taz and he was increasingly sure that he could convince her that he wasn't the rogue she imagined him to be. And then the way would be clear for them to get together—

'Jude?' she said impatiently, interrupting his thoughts.

'I'm listening.'

Down went her lashes, covering the molten brown eyes. 'I—I want to see your father,' she said in a rush.

'My...*father*?'

The disappointment hit him like a blow to the solar plexus. Equally astonished and puzzled, he reached out and pushed back her tousled hair so that he could see her face more clearly. Her solemn gaze distracted him. He let his fingers linger at her ear, moving them slowly down her beautiful neck to rest gently on her trembling shoulder.

'Why?' he asked huskily.

She looked up at him and his heart stood still, his blood pounding turgidly in his body. 'I want to make peace between us all,' she whispered.

Hypnotised by her liquid gaze, he struggled to keep hold of the plot. Her eyes shone with hope and all his control evaporated. Without stopping to think of the consequences he drew her close and brushed her lips with his. At least, he meant to. Somehow it turned into a full-blown kiss and she was responding passionately, making little moans of pleasure in her throat, her mouth soft and yielding beneath his onslaught.

Her mouth opened in surprise and he slid the tip of his tongue experimentally between her lips and teased his way in, tasting her sweetness, exploring the erotic moistness and letting his self-control slip dangerously away.

This was it. His salvation, his way out of hell.

'Bel—'

'Doesn't love me, remember?'

He could see her hesitating, a light in her eyes as if she thought she'd now be able to dissuade her stepmother from continuing with such an arrangement. But he didn't want her to think, not while her delectable mouth was inches away and so patently desperate for his attentions.

With intense concentration he kissed her temples, mouth and throat. His hand dragged at the slashed neckline of the T-shirt to bare her shoulder.

'Beautiful,' he whispered, lightly grazing his teeth over the gleaming skin.

'No,' she mumbled indistinctly. 'Belinda!'

And he found himself saying with absolute finality, 'It's over. All over.'

'*Jude!*'

Her head rolled from side to side, her abandon and high state of arousal exciting him beyond belief. She clutched at him as if she, too, had been celibate for years. When he pushed his hands beneath her shirt he discovered that she wore no bra. He groaned as his fingers touched the firm swell of her voluptuous breasts and when he caressed each throbbing nipple she cried out then gripped a handful of his hair and brought his mouth down hard on hers, her body shuddering with every move of his fingers.

'*Dios!*' he muttered, driven beyond all rationality.

Scooping her up, he carried her in hard and fast strides to her bedroom where he set her on the bed, his eyes coal-black and burning as he contemplated her trembling, expectant body.

He was mad to believe this meant anything to her. Sex and titillation were the breath of life to her. He was taking one hell of a risk. By abandoning Belinda and turning to Taz, he could be throwing away everything he'd worked for all these years.

His stomach cramped. If she walked out on him after this, claiming it had only been a casual encounter, he'd never forgive her. She couldn't do that to him, not when he felt like this.

Hating himself for wanting her so much, he lowered himself to her, breathing her in, desperately kissing every inch of her face and throat. Then his mouth moved to her breasts, each one infinitely warm and perfumed, the nipples engorged and tantalising between his lips while his hands inexorably worked at the fastenings of her shorts and eased them down her writhing hips. Taz moaned and protested but encouraged him with her hands, her mouth, and her body.

His fingers encountered thin silk, luxurious and slippery to the touch. Mindlessly she kissed and nibbled his shoulder, her teeth digging in as she urged him on with breathless little pleas.

Nothing could stop him now. His eyes closed in ecstasy when he discovered that she was hot and wet and equally desperate. Her entire body jerked in pleasure as he gently brought her to the peak of arousal.

A shudder passed through his entire length. Abandoning himself to his folly, he kissed her long and hard and slid into her, feeling her warmth close around him, her strong muscles gripping him in an unbearably exquisite torture.

Their bodies and his intensely primal desire for Taz bound Jude's whole world at that moment and nothing, no one else existed.

Despite knowing she was without morals or honour he wanted to devour every inch, to hold her so tightly that she became part of him and to make love to her like this for hour after hour. She seemed as insatiable as he was. Naked and slicked with sweat, they moved in an increasingly hectic rhythm, kissing, suckling and moaning with the sheer relief of released sexual energy.

Jude began to feel his mind disintegrating. The sound of her voice became far-away and a roaring in his ears obliterated everything till there was only one place that existed: the core of her body, the hard thrusting of his. He cried out hoarsely, his eyes opening at the spasms rippling through him from head to toe in wave upon wave.

Taz was looking at him, her beautiful dark eyes bright with tears, and she was whispering his name too, jerkily, because her body was clenching him powerfully and, even in his dazed state, he realised that he was experiencing not only his orgasm, but hers as well.

For incredible minutes the climax continued till he thought he might die of pleasure. And then there was just a rolling warmth flowing through him, and after that came a wonderful, blissful calm.

CHAPTER FIVE

DEEPLY content, Taz lay in the cradle of Jude's arms, every knotted muscle in her body now relaxed and at rest. She let herself drift as if she were floating in a warm sea and oddly weightless, as if her bones didn't exist.

Jude began to kiss her, slowly at first, beginning with the soles of her feet and then her toes, moving on to her ankles... She shuddered, her senses reeling again as he pinned her arms to the bed, forcing her to remain still while he expertly sensitised every inch of her skin till she felt a deeper, more visceral throbbing inside her.

But he denied her any satisfaction. Driven wild by his languorous torment, her body was juddering uncontrollably before he gave in to her hoarse demands. And even then he tantalised her with long, slow strokes of exquisite pleasure as he took her on the long journey to mutual release.

'Taz! Taz!' he muttered thickly, burying his face in her neck.

She held him, delirious with delight and stunned by his passion. It had been so long since she'd felt so much at peace. After a while she realised that he had fallen asleep but she lay awake, letting the silence and pleasure flow over her like an incoming tide until her thoughts began to touch on reality again.

And gradually doubts began to obliterate the sensation of serenity from her mind and body. Beside her, Jude breathed steadily, a slight smile on his face. Contented...or smug? She wasn't sure.

Oh, God! What had she done?

How had it happened? She had a dim recollection of being kissed and then totally losing control. Taz cringed, shrinking away from Jude's warm body as she examined her behaviour—and his. He'd made love to her but hadn't spoken any loving words. There'd been nothing to suggest that this had been anything more than a one-night stand.

She felt herself grow hot with humiliation. He'd treated her like an easy pick-up—and she'd behaved like one, giving in to the explosion of need without a thought for the consequences.

It was because she still loved him, she thought hopelessly. And always would. Nothing else, only that remorseless, insistent love, could have allowed her to temporarily lose her sanity and her awareness of the difference between right and wrong.

She held her breath, horribly aware of Jude's relaxed, naked body close beside her own, taut form. Once he'd accused her of being promiscuous. Her eagerness to jump into bed with him after a brief reacquaintance would have reinforced that impression.

What price her integrity now? How could he ever treat her with respect again?

She bit her lip to stop a groan emerging, her body now rigid with dismay. She'd been very, very stupid and Jude had every reason to despise her. She despised herself enough as it was.

Jude muttered something in his sleep and she stiffened as his arm came to curl around her. Its weight was like an iron band, imprisoning her.

They couldn't stay here like this. Belinda might come back any moment! Feeling hysterical, she stealthily edged away. His hand slid to her breast and she saw his mouth curve into an even more contented smile. Even in her panic she felt like kissing his sleepy mouth.

She'd got it bad, she thought gloomily, and wriggled towards the extreme edge of the bed, an inch at a time, hardly daring to breathe in case she woke him.

But she had to escape before Belinda arrived. He'd said

the relationship was over and there was no love between him and her stepmother, but it would be a shock to be dumped, nevertheless. Bel obviously needed a man like Jude to look after her.

This was a mess. Taz felt terrible. She tried to console herself with the fact that at least the engagement was over, and that Jude's behaviour had shown he wasn't ready for marriage and fidelity. Perhaps the news wouldn't be too devastating under the circumstances, since Bel didn't love him.

She lay still, turning this thought over and over in her mind because something didn't quite tally. Then Taz went cold as she suddenly remembered the passion in her stepmother's voice when she'd talked about her lover. Someone wasn't telling the truth—and Bel had no reason to lie.

Taz licked her dry lips, staring huge-eyed into space. Could he have lied to her? He'd coaxed her into bed on the strength of the fact that he was, essentially, a free man. But she only had his word for that and bitter experience should have told her that his word had little value.

Her skin began to crawl as a dreadful suspicion began to make itself known. Had he been truthful about Belinda's feelings? He'd lied before so she knew she couldn't trust him. Why had she believed him so readily this time?

A horrible sensation coiled hotly in the pit of her stomach. She couldn't fool herself. In her heart of hearts she'd known what that kiss would lead to because Jude wasn't the kind of man to leave his arousal unsatisfied.

But she'd wanted him so badly that she'd been prepared to accept anything he said, if it then freed her to indulge in her desires with a clear conscience.

And Jude would have known that. He'd deceived her, she was sure of it. She lay quite numb, trying to make her sluggish brain work, and slowly she began to take in the enormity of what she had done. Almost certainly she had betrayed her stepmother's trust in the most shocking way.

She shuddered, her whole body cramped with misery.

Suddenly, utterly repelled by her behaviour, she felt the need to escape. She was unable to bear the thought of being near him a second longer. Finally she was free.

Almost weeping with distress, she silently slid a sleeveless white dress from a hanger and spent an age slowly opening the drawer, which contained fresh underwear. Each squeak of the drawer made her glance in terror towards his sleeping figure.

At last she reached the safety of the bathroom and shut the door. Here she showered, scrubbing her detested body so hard that she emerged a startling pink. Then she roughly dried herself and dressed in a frantic but silent hurry, her fingers shaking so much that she could hardly cope. And she grimly avoided any glimpse of her own horrified and guilty face in the huge gilt mirror.

She felt deeply ashamed. At the price of great sex, she'd surrendered every last scrap of moral decency she possessed. She'd slept with her stepmother's lover. It was the worst thing she could ever have done.

As for Jude, whatever his feelings, he'd had no right, no *right* to touch another woman!

Her face contorted in hatred and she swayed, holding onto the edge of the washbasin as the nausea hit her.

She couldn't bear it. In one awful morning, he'd stripped away every ounce of her self-respect and had turned her into nothing more than a lust-crazed animal. She felt terrible, *terrible*. She'd never forget this, never forgive him or herself.

Taz moaned, blaming herself for everything. She'd been arrogant to think that she could outwit him. He'd used sex as a weapon to hurt her and Belinda, and to assert his superiority.

She stopped dead, her eyes widening in horror as something awful occurred to her. Perhaps this was part of his planned punishment for them! Could he be that malevolent? Could he have set out deliberately to seduce them both?

It would be the ultimate triumph—sexual domination of the two Laker women, showing his deep contempt for them. He'd tricked her into bed long ago by professing undying love. He was calculating enough to use lies to seduce her again.

She let out a low groan. Yes. It was possible. Jude honoured and revered his father with a passion that transcended everything.

Taz felt overwhelmed with remorse and anger that she'd allowed herself to get into this dreadful situation. Sickness raked relentlessly at her stomach as she tiptoed across the bedroom carpet and she felt petrified that Jude might wake.

Halfway across the living room beyond, she heard the voice she was dreading.

'Leaving so soon?'

His harsh and bitter tone paralysed her. There was no softness there, only a sneering derision which confirmed her fears. He didn't sound like a man who'd found the woman of his dreams.

She'd been right. He'd made love to her out of spite. And, fool that she was, she'd fallen for his smooth talk a second time.

Without turning, she summoned all her strength and steadied herself. 'Why not? There's nothing to stay for!' she hurled at him, feeling the anger rising to choke her.

'You *are* a sexual butterfly, aren't you?' he drawled. 'Very much the modern, independent woman.'

Unable to bear the tension, she turned and confronted him, hesitating momentarily at the sight of him leaning against the doorjamb. He was bare-chested, a sheet hitched around his hard, lean hips. Her stupid heart lurched and she loathed herself even more.

'You've got me wrong. I'm leaving because I'm regretting that I let you paw me!'

'You wanted me,' he growled, his expression menacing.

'I wanted *it*!' she corrected, knowing as she said it that

this was a wild distortion of the truth. But she was pleased to see that the barb had wounded his insufferable male pride.

'Glad to have obliged,' he drawled, his eyes black with anger.

'I'm not glad! It was a mistake. I don't want it to happen again, do you understand?' she said fiercely, her throat balling up with tears.

He regarded her with steely control. He couldn't believe how cold-blooded she could be about satisfying her carnal needs. But his father had warned him before he'd had his stroke that Laker's daughter had learned deception and manipulation from a master.

And he knew how uninhibited Taz was about sex. In his mind he'd relived their lovemaking often enough over the years.

He clenched his fists. She'd made a fool of him twice! His whole being revolted at her hedonistic steam-rollering of his feelings and his pride. But she'd get her come-uppance. He'd see to that.

His eyes glittered. 'I'm satisfied for the moment. When I need sex again I'll let you know and we can come to some kind of financial arrangement if you like.'

Her head lifted proudly to hide the hurt inside her. How could she have loved him? He was evil through and through and she had to stop him from exacting any further revenge.

'I don't sell myself!' she flared.

'True.' He looked her up and down. 'You give it away for free. Fine by me.'

She wanted to cry but wouldn't give him the satisfaction. 'Never again!' she said vehemently. 'So, Jude, will you tell Belinda what has happened or shall I?'

He shrugged. 'Do as you like. She won't care.'

'You're bluffing!' she scathed. 'I don't believe a word you say! Do you think she's made of stone? If she gets to hear of this it'll crucify her, you unfeeling, callous—!'

'I am none of those! I told you, she doesn't love me!' he interrupted irascibly.

'Well, forgive me if I wait to hear that from her own lips!' she replied hotly. 'I remember the tenderness in her voice when she said she'd fallen madly in love and that she had a lover—'

'Tenderness?'

'It wasn't faked,' she said doggedly.

'Then it wasn't me but someone else she was talking about!'

He was very still now, staring at her from beneath his lowered brows. A lover. Could that be Harvey? His heart began to thud. If he could be sure...

He knew what he would do. Make Bel admit it so he could be free. And he'd seduce Taz again, make her beg for him, make her dependent on him. Marry her.

Then, once he had control of the hospital, he'd tell her that emotionally and mentally she left him cold. She had to learn she couldn't treat men and sex so casually.

'Perhaps,' he continued, 'Bel only appeared to be refer-ring to me—but was thinking of someone else!'

Taz wished that were true. It would make her feel better. 'You're saying that to excuse your behaviour,' she accused miserably.

'I don't excuse it,' he replied shortly. 'But I knew it wouldn't hurt her—and I presume you did too, or why would you let your stepmother's fiancé make love to you?'

Taz winced at his brutal summary of the facts. He was right. He'd sown the seeds of doubt in her mind about his relationship with Bel—perhaps deliberately—before he'd made a pass.

'I can't trust you,' she said in a low voice. 'That can't come as a huge surprise to you, Jude.'

'I dislike being bracketed with the con men and criminals you and your father consorted with,' he said grimly. 'Your standards of honesty are not mine—'

'We distrust each other,' she acknowledged with great sadness, her chest tight with choking pain.

She was desolate. And didn't understand why.

Jude's mouth was thin with disapproval, his eyes blazing beneath the lowered brows. 'You can easily discover whether I've been telling you the truth. Ask her about the arrangement we made.'

'*You* tell me,' she suggested icily. 'And I'll see if her story tallies.'

He drew in a breath as if she'd insulted him, his head held high. 'She wanted someone to look after her and keep her in the luxury to which she's become accustomed and—'

'You were to get control of the hospital,' Taz finished contemptuously. 'Only you won't, will you?' she taunted. 'You'll have to share it with me!'

A nerve flickered in his jaw. 'Never.'

Taz felt her heart begin to race. Was he planning something else? 'You have no choice unless you marry us both! Or...' She swallowed, near to tears, as she struggled to voice her worst fear. 'Or were you going to run me alongside Bel as your mistress and control us both?'

He hissed in his breath. 'You could think that of me?'

'Yes!' she cried hysterically. 'Is that why you seduced me? Did you imagine you could have your cake and your jam and enjoy all the benefits we both could provide?'

His fists were clenched, his cheekbones standing out rawly with fury. 'You have a devious and underhand mind,' he said scornfully, 'and your father would be proud of you!'

She strode over to him, her hand raised, and then she lowered it in shame that she'd briefly considered hitting him. And both the anguish in his eyes and the savage cast to his face shook her to the core.

'Keep this strictly between *us* and leave my father out of it!' she choked. 'He's dead and can't defend himself. Yours, at least, is alive and perhaps regretting his deception!'

For a moment he feared that he was close to losing control, his whole body shaking with barely contained fury. Only he knew that his father was hanging onto life because every day he hoped for retribution. He trembled with anger to think that the Lakers were still causing his father grief.

He had to be sure of Bel's feelings for Harvey—and then he could safely ease her into the man's arms. And take Taz for himself.

Taz retreated till her back hit the wall, her eyes wide with apprehension as she realised just how dangerous he might be.

'You fool so many people with your apparent sweetness and charm,' he snarled. 'But in reality you are the product of your upbringing. The daughter of an adulteress and a crook! Don't land me with the responsibility of seducing you! We both wanted sex. And, for your information, I wasn't intending to set you up as my mistress. I'm not into masochism,' he said sarcastically. 'Nor do I use sex as a weapon—just pleasure. Though, on this occasion, it's left me with a very unpleasant aftertaste.'

Hot and humiliated, Taz felt tears pricking the backs of her eyes. Her instinct was to leave before she lost face by sobbing her heart out, but there was something she had to do first.

'You can say what you like about me—I don't care what you think! But I'm going to see Belinda to tell her everything and make sure I end this travesty of a marriage!' she declared jerkily. 'You said it was over between you two but you lied! It was only a trick to seduce me!' she yelled.

'Is there any point in my denying that? You wouldn't believe me whatever I said!' he roared.

She blanched. 'You're ruthless!' she whispered, appalled. 'No sane woman on earth would get involved with you!'

His eyes kindled with a dangerous, glittering light. 'And no sane man with you. So you'd better leave, before we both lose our minds again and indulge in a little pleasurable self-torture,' he said softly.

Taz trembled from the jolt of sensual awareness that leapt across the room at her. 'God, Jude, I *hate* you!' she said brokenly, fighting the loathsome desire that was reducing her to jelly.

'The feeling's mutual!' he spat venomously. 'Now, why don't you get out of my sight before I prove to you how unstable your morals are?'

She took one look at him and fled, stumbling into the door in her desperation to leave. Jude made no move to help her as she fumbled for the handle even though he must have known she'd bruised her shoulder when she'd crashed into the door's edge.

She wouldn't allow him to inflict himself on Belinda, she vowed a few minutes later, trying hopelessly to get the car key into the lock. When she succeeded, and half fell into the driver's seat, she was appalled to see Jude's hand reaching in and snatching the keys from her shaking hand.

'You'll kill yourself if you drive off now,' he said tersely. 'The road's dangerous enough as it is, without you charging off in a temper.'

She saw that he wore just jeans and sneakers. She closed her eyes, forcing back her tears, determined that he wouldn't know how upset she was.

'Will you get out of my life?' she muttered hoarsely.

'My pleasure,' he said, oozing sarcasm. 'I'll leave the keys with the security guard. Collect them in half an hour.'

She heard him walking away. He'd been right, of course. She was in no fit state to drive, though why he should care she didn't know. She'd never seen him so angry. Perhaps no woman had ever walked out on him before.

Her face crumpled. She'd been so stupid. Jude always said whatever was necessary to get what he wanted. She'd *known* that! All those seductive murmurs, those tender glances had been aimed at her idiotically sentimental heart. He'd been aware that she wouldn't have touched him with a barge pole if he'd been spoken for.

Her gullibility was unbelievable.

Tears streamed down her cheeks. He'd made her feel about two inches high. And now she'd have to face Belinda.

She straightened and wiped her eyes. There was no way Jude was going to stay engaged. She'd put a spanner in his works.

She'd see Bel later at the apartment and tell her exactly what had happened and what kind of a low-bellied reptile her supposed fiancé was. She felt sick at the thought. There would be fireworks.

When she'd calmed down a little she collected the keys and began to drive, desperate for time and peace in which to think. Heading for the mountains, she went to her favourite spot overlooking a deep and remote valley. The cool air and silence washed over her. For two hours she tried to explain to herself how—and why—she'd let Jude make love to her when she should have known that he couldn't be trusted.

But logic didn't have anything to do with her behaviour. It had been raw and primal and, quite simply, earth-shattering. When he'd kissed her she'd thought of nothing and no one, only an all-pervading happiness.

She trembled. It had seemed, for a while, as if they were in love again. Her heart had filled with a wonderful emotion. The sex had been special because of her intense and tender feelings, which had softened all her defences.

But she had no excuse. She should have been wary, and resisted. And now came the hardest part of all: telling her stepmother what had happened.

Tentatively Taz rang the apartment bell later that afternoon, her fingers crossed in the hope that Belinda was on her own. There was no answer. Feeling she'd scaled a mountain and fallen down it again, she went to the bar, ordered *tila* and a *churro* and sat outside sipping the lime-flower drink and nibbling the hot doughnut in a desultory way, watching the entrance nervously.

The hours wore on and she began to feel ill. Realising she'd had no breakfast or lunch, she forced herself to pick at an omelette and was just spooning a drizzle of cheese onto a chunk of bread when she spotted a rather dishevelled Belinda wandering through the fake jungle.

Taz felt her stomach swoop to her fashionable sandals and wished she'd stuck to salad. But at least Bel looked radiant and glowing, which was encouraging.

'Bel!' she called, waving frantically.

Her stepmother started and flushed scarlet. 'Taz!' She hesitated, then ran over, flinging herself into Taz's arms. '*Ciao*, darling! So wonderful to see you, *chérie*! I'm sorry I wasn't around—'

'It's OK,' Taz said nervously, giving her an affectionate hug. 'I gather you and Jude had a run-in last night. Bang went your romantic dinner, I hear.'

'Oh. Yes. But…I—I stayed with a friend and we had a good time. Chatting and that, you know.'

Taz felt awful. She looked at Belinda's happy face guiltily, knowing that there would soon be tears and recriminations. But she had to face up to the consequences of her actions, however dire.

'Shall we talk upstairs?' she suggested shakily. 'I've been here ages and have only eaten an omelette.' She tried to sound normal. 'I think they'll make me apply for a residency permit if I stay any longer.'

Belinda grinned obligingly at the weak joke. 'Idiot! Oh, Taz, I'd forgotten how much fun you are and how easy it is to be with you! And you look fantastic! Where did you get that divine dress…?'

Chattering merrily, she led the way to the flat. The silent and apprehensive Taz noticed that Belinda wasn't carrying any overnight luggage and her emotions were touched. Her stepmother's exit must have been sudden and unplanned—and probably highly emotional because of the quarrel.

'You sound happy,' Taz commented, a little puzzled.

'I am,' Bel replied dreamily.

Taz felt her throat close up. This was terrible. She *could* say nothing, of course...but then she'd regret it when the marriage failed, as she knew it would. There was nothing for it.

Steeling herself, she sat next to Belinda on the settee and took hold of her hands. With a thumping heart, and with tautly strung nerves making her voice tremble, she said in a strangled voice, 'I have something to tell you, Bel. I have a terrible confession. Something awful.'

Belinda listened, her eyes widening as Taz first explained her old relationship with Jude. Something made Taz avoid any mention of Mateo's hospital scam. It didn't seem relevant and there was more than enough for Belinda to comprehend as it was.

'I have despised and hated Jude ever since, for treating me so casually,' Taz said passionately. 'He's a liar, Bel. You must understand that. But there's worse...oh, God, Bel, this is so hard!' she whispered. 'The hardest thing I've ever done! I just don't know how to tell you—'

'He's already phoned me,' Belinda broke in quickly. 'I gather you both met last night. He—he said that he told you I didn't love him.'

'Yes!' Taz felt terribly upset and a sob erupted from her throat. 'That's right.'

Belinda's tone hardened. 'I'm furious with him! He had no right to say that!'

'I know,' mumbled Taz miserably. 'It was a dreadful lie. A ploy—'

'He also told me what happened next.'

'What...? You mean...'

'You had sex,' Bel said bluntly.

Taz stared at her in astonishment, her face flaming with

heat. 'You...*knew*? You greeted me and hugged me and chatted and...you knew all along?' she cried, twisting her hands in distraction.

'I knew.'

She felt utterly confused. Belinda looked perfectly understanding, as if she knew what an uncontrollable passion could do to someone sane and normal. Taz's teeth bit into her lower lip. That was so, of course. She would know—because she must be crazy about Jude. But why was she so unmoved by his infidelity?

Had he coaxed her round? Made light of it? She frowned, realising how clever he'd been to get to Belinda first, confess, and beg her forgiveness. He was a very devious and sly man, she thought gloomily.

'I...I can't tell you how dreadful I feel,' Taz said wretchedly. 'I did actually believe that it was over between the two of you or I'd never have... Oh, Bel, I know that I was foolish, but I was pleased when he told me he was calling it off. My first thought was that if you really didn't care about him and the engagement was over, then you were safe from making a dreadful mistake...and—and then—'

'He kissed you and you couldn't think rationally.' Solemn-faced, Bel patted her hand and then squeezed it. 'It doesn't matter. Please don't be upset. I understand—'

Taz raised tragic eyes, unable to cope with being forgiven so easily. 'You shouldn't!' she wailed. 'You can't! You ought to be screaming at me and throwing things! I know what he must mean to you—'

'I said, it doesn't matter,' her stepmother repeated softly. 'Don't punish yourself. I don't care what happened. I told him that.'

Taz hardly heard, her remorse was so deep. 'I'll never forgive myself. But if I acted stupidly, well...he's a heel, Bel! He deliberately seduced me. I beg you, don't treat this lightly—'

'I know all about Jude.' Sober-faced, Belinda patted Taz's

hand again. 'He's never made a secret of what he thinks and feels. He did say that we should break our engagement because of what happened, but I'm determined to marry him nevertheless.'

Taz gaped. 'But that's crazy! He'll hurt you!' she wailed in exasperation. 'You must reconsider! You can't ever trust him, not after what he's done!'

'I can and I will. Don't interfere, darling,' Bel pleaded. 'I *need* him—'

'No!' Taz cried, aghast. 'I can't let you make such a mistake. I won't ever, ever let him touch me again, but surely you must see—'

'Stop!' Belinda cried, covering her ears. 'I won't listen! You don't understand! Leave me alone! I don't care what he's done! It doesn't matter!'

Taz put her face in her hands and groaned at her stepmother's obsessive love for a man who didn't deserve it.

'I feel even worse,' she said brokenly. 'If you forgive him so readily then you must love him to distraction.'

Belinda stared, her lower lip suddenly wobbling. 'Oh, Taz!' she wailed. 'This marriage is so important to me! You don't know how important! Don't rock the boat, please, *please*!' she wailed.

'I can't believe you can be so—'

'Stop it! I can't bear to talk about it any longer!' Bel shrieked.

Taz put her arms around her hysterical stepmother, her heart sinking because it was obvious that no amount of persuasion would make any difference. The smooth-talking Jude had taken a chance and pretended to do the decent thing in breaking off the engagement, knowing full well that Bel was too besotted to agree. So he would get what he wanted.

Her only hope was a faint one: to appeal to Mateo Corderro and get him to stop his son from wasting his life on this mockery of a marriage. Other than that, her hands were tied.

A sense of depression swamped her, making her feel very tired. She'd been worse than useless in protecting her stepmother from Jude's vengeance. And Belinda would one day pay the price. But she could do nothing more at the moment if her stepmother's mind was set.

'Hush. For your sake I won't discuss the matter for the moment,' she said jerkily. 'But you must accept that I can't stay here,' she added, totally unnerved by the prospect of seeing Jude's triumphant face whenever he called at the apartment. 'I have to find somewhere else to live.' She lifted her forlorn face to Belinda's and saw that she was looking vastly relieved.

'There's a vacant flat in the hospital,' Belinda suggested with crushing eagerness. 'It's not much, but—'

'I'll take it. Now.' Quite drained, Taz put her hand on Bel's arm, unable to go without at least a warning. 'Take care. Don't get hurt,' she said unhappily. 'He—'

'Don't worry. I know what I'm doing!' Belinda said hastily.

'OK,' she whispered, defeated. But she very much doubted it. 'I'll take my things now. Be in touch.'

'No. If you don't mind, Taz...I won't! You understand?'

Taz winced. But it was perhaps the right punishment. 'Dear Bel. I am so sorry. You've always turned to me and I'll always be there for you, if you want to talk.' Her voice broke. 'I do understand why you don't want to see me, but...don't cut yourself off from people who care about you and you alone!'

Belinda looked uneasy. 'I think it's best if we stay away from one another for a while,' she said carefully.

Taz gave a small sob and immediately the two women clung to one another, weeping. And then Taz withdrew, wiped her eyes and collected her luggage.

'Bye, darling,' she choked, hugging her tiny stepmother hard. 'Let me know if...'

'Go.' Belinda sniffed. And turned away in dismissal.

* * *

When she'd moved into the small, rather hot flat near the top of the hospital, the depressed Taz wandered around the impressive building for want of anything else to do. Her spirits lifted a little when she spotted a rather harassed-looking Harvey Hoskin, the hospital manager, walking out of an imposing office.

'Taz! This...this is a surprise—oh, hell!' he muttered when his phone rang. 'Excuse me. Don't go.'

She fidgeted, waiting while he tried to persuade a nursing agency to look for two more experienced night staff. 'Having problems?' she asked sympathetically, when he put the phone down and ran a hand through his already messed-up hair.

'Several. I could give you a list. We're short of good-quality nurses. I don't know what I'm going to do—'

'I could work here!' she cried, and blinked, startled by her offer. Then she realised that it could be the answer to her woes. 'I was a staff nurse in the intensive care unit of the neuro ward in Madrid,' she said earnestly. 'I love nursing, Harvey, and I need something to do. I'm not the sort to sit around all day and have my nails manicured. I—'

'Could you start now?' he asked. 'The problem is that we've got a bit of a cash-flow problem at the moment and I can't offer you the right wage—'

'Harvey,' she said wryly, 'money is not a problem for me at the moment. That's not why I want to work. If you want to check on my credentials then do so.'

The phone rang again and he ignored it while she ran through her previous experience.

'We need someone here desperately,' he said. 'You're just the sort of steadying influence we want. I could release someone less experienced in ICU and you could take his or her place. What about it? Is now OK?'

A happier calm was already enfolding her at the prospect of working again and she realised it was just what she needed to forget Jude and her own reprehensible behaviour.

'I'm all yours,' she said solemnly.

'Wonderful!'

Full of enthusiasm, Harvey caught her arm and led her to the small ward, which seemed to be in chaos. He organised a uniform for her and she listened carefully while procedures were explained and then she began to read each patient's notes with great care.

As each day passed she became more and more immersed in her job, working far beyond normal hours. There were problems with staff, supplies and equipment and she and Harvey worked constantly to keep the wards running. He was truly devoted to his job and she admired and liked him enormously, particularly his kind and gentle nature which seemed to ease the greatest crises.

But she worried about Belinda and she thought of Jude often when she wasn't working—and perhaps that was why she gave herself so little leisure time. She wondered what he was doing and whether he and Bel were finalising plans for their wedding...or were already married.

Whenever she thought of them together she felt sick with nerves. There was something seriously wrong with their relationship, something odd, and she knew it would turn into a disaster.

But, despite all her efforts, she'd been unable to trace Mateo's whereabouts. All she knew was that the Corderros had lived in a huge villa in Puerto Banus, but they'd moved and had left no forwarding address. Taz was beginning to realise that time was running out.

She supposed that Jude and Bel were adults and they had made their choices, but she still grieved for the loss of her stepmother's friendship. And she loathed the idea of Jude succeeding in his cold-blooded revenge.

And then, amazingly, early one morning she saw him with her stepmother and Harvey outside an apartment block near Marbella's bus station.

She'd been shopping for groceries, and was surprised be-

cause Belinda had never been keen on getting up before ten
o'clock—and also because the three of them were arguing.
Belinda seemed to be ill and unable to keep her balance,
and Jude was shouting at Harvey.

Eventually Jude bundled Belinda into his car which was
parked outside the apartments and she watched them drive
off, a puzzled frown on her face.

Her eyes met Harvey's across the street and he went
bright red. She crossed the road. 'What on earth happened?'
she asked anxiously.

'We...I can't tell you,' he said, looking panic-stricken.
'It's...they're talking things over. They often have argu-
ments. She comes to me as a friend and—and he resents it.
He's pretty annoyed this time.'

'I see,' she said doubtfully. 'Harvey, I'm really worried
about her—'

'Don't waste your breath.' He swallowed, his expression
bleak. 'We can't do anything to change the situation...'

'You care about her, don't you?' she said suddenly.

Harvey gave a mirthless laugh. 'Care? I love her, very
much,' he muttered. 'The path of true love never runs
straight, does it? Mine's littered with obstacles.'

And hers with one huge crater. 'I'm so sorry,' she said,
feeling infinitely sad. Harvey and Bel were ideally suited.
What a shame. Suddenly she had a burning desire to end
the farce of this marriage once and for all. 'If only I could
speak to his father,' she said, voicing her thoughts aloud, 'I
might be able to stop them. But I've tried the apartment in
Banus where the Corderros used to live, and have drawn a
blank.'

'Well, that wasn't their main residence,' explained Harvey, then clamped his mouth shut in an odd way, as if he'd
said too much.

She looked at him, her hopes rising. 'How would you
know?'

'I...I had dealings with them when I was a junior legal

assistant in one of your father's businesses,' he said, his face flushing pink.

'You're brilliant! Tell me where he might live, then!' she begged.

'I forget.'

He was lying. Why? His reticence exasperated her. 'Think, Harvey! It's important! You must remember. You've the best memory of anyone I know!'

'It's...oh, a farm somewhere beyond Alta Zahara,' he said vaguely, 'though it's probably been sold off by now. They had money troubles.'

'And where was this farm?' she demanded.

Harvey shifted his feet. 'Past Ronda. Some remote valley.'

'Thanks,' she said warmly. 'I'll go there and make enquiries when my next shift's over.'

Somehow, with Harvey's help, Belinda must be persuaded that she'd never be happy with a man who was using her.

She wished now that she'd explained to her stepmother about Jude's obsession in getting his hands on the hospital. By chickening out of telling the unpleasant truth, she'd only prolonged a distressing and volatile relationship—and the truth would have to be told eventually.

Taz sighed. She'd got it totally wrong. She'd tried to spare Bel and, in doing so, had made things worse. They'd probably chosen their bridesmaids now. Pink or purple? she thought, trying to raise a smile, but a pang sliced through her heart and Harvey caught her arm.

'Forget him. You'd be wasting your time. The old man's as stubborn as a mule. I'll take you to work, shall I?' he said lightly.

'Thanks. And...don't worry. Between us we'll make sure she's OK,' she said.

And, despite Harvey's advice, she began to plan what she'd say to Mateo and how she'd get Belinda somewhere quiet and private, and tell her the whole story. She might be heartbroken to begin with, but better that—and coping with the consequences—than greater anguish later, when they were married and Jude was treating Bel like dirt.

What a fool she'd been, Taz mused. Trying to be kind could have devastating repercussions. Sometimes tough love was better.

Subdued and thoughtful, she started her shift. And soon she was in the world she adored, and finding that a great weight had been lifted from her shoulders. She was even able to share jokes with the patients and to cheer up their anxious visitors.

Whatever mistakes she made in the outside world—even if her heart was in the right place and she'd been well-meaning—the hospital was where her skills and judgement never let her down. This was where she'd concentrate her life, where caring for the sick and needy gave her a sense of achievement and fed her empty heart.

How sad it was that Jude had become hard and ruthless. He was allowing his head to rule his heart. One day he'd find himself in trouble and discover that unselfish and pure love was more important than anything else.

CHAPTER SIX

HE'D driven away with Belinda in the car feeling angrier than he'd ever been in his life. *Both* of the Laker women had been playing him for a sucker!

Taz had used him to ease her voracious sexual appetite—and perhaps to underline the fact that she was calling the shots because she was obviously a control freak—and Belinda had been sleeping with Harvey, while all the time she'd been insisting that the marriage of convenience go ahead!

It was incredible! The two women were pathologically immoral, devious, deceitful... He ground his teeth together. They'd regret their nasty little schemes. Now he had no compunction whatsoever where they were concerned. Emotion would not rule him again.

Shaking with fury, he drove with intense concentration, hardly aware of the sobbing Belinda beside him. She was history. His energies must now be turned to Taz.

Deep within his body, his sexual hunger leapt into life. His breathing became rapid and he knew that his revenge would take the form of sexual domination—and then rejection, once he had his hands securely on the hospital.

He thought of making love to Taz, of possessing her lush, mobile body once more and kissing her soft, yielding mouth. This was a revenge he'd enjoy to the full, every last, sizzling second.

Cold to the heart, his expression bleak and his feelings carefully protected behind an impenetrable shield, he began to tell Belinda that their arrangement was over once and for all.

He heard Belinda yell something unintelligible, and shot

116

a quick glance at her distorted face. She began to scream at him and then she was lashing out while he tried desperately to avoid her and yet retain control of the car.

She grabbed the wheel and jerked it violently to the right. A fraction too late he grabbed it, braked and shouted a warning as they hurtled towards the barrier. And then there was just darkness.

It seemed only a short time later that he was groggily dragging himself from an uneasy and unnatural sleep. Gradually he began to realise that something wasn't quite right.

For some strange reason he couldn't open his eyes—and his body seemed to be moving even though he was convinced that he was lying still. A dream, then, he decided hazily.

A strong and cloying perfume assailed his nostrils and he grimaced in disgust then felt a searing pain in his face and head.

At that moment a woman shrieked in his ear and began to paw him. He wanted to avoid her but, in the dream, his entire body had become paralysed. Everything hurt. His muscles felt as though he'd exercised each one individually to exhaustion, his bones ached and it was as though knives were being driven into his head. Thankfully, the shrieking receded and he felt himself drifting away into oblivion.

Later—he didn't know when—he woke again to the same immobility and the same darkness, but this time he heard a distant voice he recognised.

Taz's.

He supposed he was hallucinating or in some terrible nightmare because his eyes remained obstinately shut. But he wanted to end the dream.

'Taz!' he mumbled incoherently.

This time he inhaled a pleasant and natural scent of freshly scrubbed hands and newly shampooed hair. A firm and gentle hand enclosed his, bringing instant peace to his panicking brain.

'Taz?' he whispered again through painfully bruised lips.

'I'm here,' she said miraculously. 'Keep your oxygen mask on, Jude. Glad you're back with us.'

Not understanding, he frowned, and it hurt. Something—presumably the oxygen mask—settled around his nose and mouth and he could feel elastic biting into his cheek for a moment, before something softer, like cotton wool, was tucked beneath it.

Taz rested a hand lightly on his brow and he felt a wonderful sense of calm despite the irritating peeping sound somewhere on his right side.

'Frowning isn't the best thing you could choose to do at the moment,' she advised gently. 'Your head isn't up to coping with facial expressions. Jude, can you understand what I'm saying?'

'Y-y-ye-e-es,' he croaked, bewildered.

What was wrong with his head? He struggled to think. He remembered being in his car with Belinda. There'd been an argument. She'd been drunk. What had happened? He became aware that Taz was speaking and tried hard to concentrate.

'Jude? Jude? I want you to listen to me… That's better. You've had an accident,' she said, slowly and clearly. 'You're in hospital and you'll be all right but you've had a bang on the head. Do you understand?'

'Am I awake?' he asked, appalled at his feeble voice.

And he clung tightly to her hand as if it were a lifeline. He felt safe with her. Reassured. He inhaled deeply and instantly felt light-headed from the oxygen.

'More or less. You feel dazed and confused, I expect. And you'll have a terrible headache in time. But I'm real enough,' she said, squeezing his hand in return, as if she knew that he couldn't be sure of that. 'This isn't a dream,

Jude, or I wouldn't be able to feel my bones being turned to dust by your crushing grip!'

He tried to smile but it hurt, though he realised she wouldn't be joking with him if he were seriously ill. Cheered, he relaxed even more and heard the peeping sound fade to nothing.

Trying to sound matter-of-fact, he concealed his panic and said, 'I can't see. Are there bandages over my eyes?'

'No,' she said gently. 'They're bruised and swollen from the impact and you look as if you've been down an alley with ten prize fighters, but we'll get the swelling down soon and your sight will be spot-on again.'

He tried to take this in. 'We? And what impact?'

'The accident, remember? You and Belinda were in a car crash. If you don't recall it, that's not unusual. Your memory will almost certainly return. And I'm working as a staff nurse at the Laker Hospital now.'

'The Laker Hospital?' he repeated drily. 'They've put me in the *Laker Hospital*?'

''Fraid so. It's a bit ironic, isn't it? But Bel insisted. She's OK, by the way. A few bruises, that's all.'

He listened to her listing his injuries. A fracture of the skull, concussion, and some internal bleeding and severe bruising.

'I sound a mess,' he commented hoarsely.

'You are. I didn't recognise you when you turned up. Still, it won't be long before you're pretty again. Don't worry. I haven't lost anyone in your condition yet and I don't intend to start now.'

He tried again to understand what she'd said but he couldn't think straight. Was it his imagination or had she sounded shaky?

'What...happened?' he said with difficulty.

'We don't know yet. It's not important at the moment. Harvey's talking to Bel now. I want you to rest and—and thank your lucky stars you're alive.'

He felt moisture on the back of his hand. Taz swept it away. He tried desperately to open his eyes and to see why her voice had become hoarse, and why she was coughing.

'Ugh!' he groaned, as a wave of pain crashed through his head and the bleeps set up a frenzied concert.

'Try to relax,' she whispered gently. 'Your job is to lie there and do nothing. We nurses need *someone* to practise on, you know.'

'So I've been dragged in here purely for your amusement?' he grunted painfully.

'That's better,' she soothed. 'Accept your role gladly. If you're good I'll allow you a lovely liquid feed.'

His screaming muscles unknotted with his tentative smile. 'I'd rather have a shot of manzanilla,' he mumbled sleepily.

'You'll get water and like it,' she said, pretending to scold him. 'It'll be a long while before you can have anything as exciting as alcohol.'

He drifted, thinking how pleasant it would be to sit with her on La Quinta's terrace—'My father!' he cried suddenly, trying to sit up. As she gently eased him back, he said anxiously, 'Taz, he'll be worried—'

'It's all right,' she reassured him. 'We found your home number on your mobile and contacted him. Well, not him exactly—no one would let us disturb him—but Harvey spoke to someone called Carmen who said she'd relay the message.'

Yes. She could be relied on to cope, he thought. And everyone at La Quinta would rally round and support his father. Thank God for warm-hearted friends. He sensed that she was beginning to move away and suddenly he felt vulnerable.

'Stay with me! I can't see, I don't know what's going on—'

'Of course.'

He hadn't imagined it. Her voice had trembled. He

frowned, trying to work out why. And he felt a deep tiredness washing up his entire body.

Taz could hardly bear to look at his damaged face. The surgeons had shaven part of his head but a pressure bandage hid this. The area around his eye sockets was a startling dense black as if it had been painted with bitumen and she knew that his face would soon turn purple and then yellow from the impact. His lips had bled, his beautiful nose was broken and there was a terrible gash on his cheekbone.

For the first time in her life, as she'd checked the computer read-outs after he'd come up from the theatre, she'd wanted to rush off and howl her eyes out over a patient. The shock of seeing him arrive on the ward, accompanied by an incoherent Belinda, had made her press her hand deep into her stomach to prevent herself from vomiting.

As it was, she'd uttered a silent scream that had strained her vocal cords and left her shaking uncontrollably until Harvey had sat her down and made her breathe deeply.

She had feared brain damage. She'd known so many young people come in as trauma cases and, inside, she had privately wept for them and their families. What would Jude be like when he woke? She couldn't bear it if he'd suffered permanent brain injury, with that brilliant mind gone for ever.

He was too young, she kept protesting. So much of his life ahead of him. How lucky everyone was who'd never known this dreadful fear, this awful period of waiting and uncertainty. And how terrible for those families who had to face the awful truth that their loved ones would never be the same again.

She couldn't settle. She couldn't eat. She trembled all the time. Despite being off-duty, every waking second for two hours she'd stayed by his bed, willing him to be his normal, unpleasant self. When he'd spoken her name, somehow identifying her by touch alone, she'd been overjoyed.

Taz shut her eyes, close to surrendering to an all-enveloping darkness. He was over the first hurdle. Nothing else seemed to matter any more. Not even her injured pride over Jude's rejection all those years ago, or the fact that he'd put duty before anything else, or even her own shame in betraying Belinda. They had become minor problems in the face of Jude's condition. Con man he might be, liar, seducer, cold-blooded manipulator...but he was hurt and in pain and she wouldn't have wished that on anyone, least of all Jude.

He was still seriously ill and on the danger list till the bleeding in his brain stopped. She felt the breath drying in her throat with fear as she wrote up his chart and she had to wipe her eyes because they were too bleary for her to see.

Please let him live, she prayed, over and over again, only too aware of the complications that could arise in a case like this. Automatically she carried out her duties, forcing herself to act normally. But he was constantly on her mind.

And when she took a break she went to the little chapel on the top floor of the hospital and could think only of him, of happier times, as she sat in the pew, her fingers twisting and fussing continually in her lap.

The memories came thick and fast as if her mind had stored away images in a reference library. She drew in a long, shuddering breath. They'd shared so many wonderful moments.

Like on their first date, eating garlicky prawns in a poppy field with the sound of goat bells coming from the hills above them...

Sunlight drenching his face as they had lain in a grove of orange-blossom where he'd just kissed her and had declared his undying love two weeks later...

The glistening of diamond droplets on his incredible body as he'd stood in swimming trunks beneath a small waterfall, the snow-capped Sierra a distant and dazzling whiteness on the horizon. They'd been going out for two months and on that day he'd stepped from under the waterfall and had beckoned her to join him.

'You'll be safe with me. I'll take care of you,' he'd coaxed, when she'd hesitated, knowing what must inevitably follow if she obeyed him and dived into the inviting pool. 'Come to me, Taz. I love you so much I can't wait any longer,' he'd said softly.

In her mind's eye, Taz watched the whole course of her time with Jude, reliving every moment hungrily. Only now that his life was in danger did she realise how deeply she had loved him. And part of her must still cherish those carefree, happy days—even though they had been a sham—because she felt devastated to think that he might be suffering now.

She jumped up and began to walk up and down the small church, unable to remain still for a moment. Harvey had forced her to take this break, saying she needed it, but her eyes constantly went to the hands on her watch, which moved more slowly than she could have believed possible.

Although she saw Jude clearly for what he was, she didn't hate him any more. With all her heart she wanted him to live, to be well and without pain. Her anguished eyes closed and she sank into a pew, praying as she'd never prayed before.

Let him live. Let him recover his mind totally. But, above all, let him *live*!

A hand touched her shoulder and she turned to see the priest gazing at her in concern. 'What troubles you, Taz?' he asked. 'Are you worrying too much for your patients and their relatives?'

Her eyes filled with tears. The priest had seen her sitting with grieving relatives on several occasions when she'd tried to offer strength and consolation to them.

'It's someone—a patient—I know,' she said jerkily. 'Someone I...was very close to.'

The priest held her hand and said nothing but his presence

helped. Calmer now, she wondered how her hatred for Jude could have been wiped away by the accident. Unless she'd never hated him at all.

Maybe she'd been angry instead, because she'd been unable to have what she craved more than anything in the world: Jude himself, flaws and all. Though, in her heart of hearts, she knew he'd treat her badly because he was totally untrustworthy.

But how unimportant her anger seemed now! 'We had a row,' she told the listening priest. 'And now all I want is for him to get well.'

'Then you are fortunate,' he said gently. 'You can take practical steps to ensure he does. Trust in God and the healing process, Taz.'

She smiled at him through her tears. 'Yes,' she said. 'Thank you. I'll do everything I can. Everything.'

When she returned to the ward she checked his read-outs. High BP. Pulse too fast. Her hand came to settle on his and she willed him to relax.

'Taz,' he mumbled, looking drawn and weak.

'I'm here,' she said chokily.

'Stay.'

A smile touched his pained mouth. Her hand increased its pressure and she was overjoyed when his fingers slowly curled around hers.

'I have to ask you some questions. Do you know where you are?' she asked, shaking with emotion.

'Hospital. Will you nurse me personally?' he asked, gripping her hand fiercely.

'I'll be on the ward all the time,' she assured him. 'What year is it?'

'Don't you know?' he jerked wryly.

Smiling through misty eyes, she ran through her bank of questions to establish his acuity and then began to test his reflexes. 'I have to do this every hour,' she explained. 'Day and night. You'll get fed up with me soon. Do you remember what happened yet?'

He scowled, and winced. 'Yes. Bel—'

'Don't worry. I told you: she's unhurt but shocked,' Taz said quickly. 'She—she was desperately worried about you.'

'I don't want to see her!'

'But—!'

'No!'

'Hush! You've made everything beep!' she scolded gently. 'If you don't want her to see you like this, I understand. You're not at your most handsome! And you're right, she'd be terribly upset at the way you look. I'll say you were asking after her, shall I? She—she does love you, Jude.'

His jaw tightened but he felt too weak to argue, drifting in and out of sleep only to be woken periodically by those idiotic questions. When he felt better, he'd tell Taz what had happened. For the minute he was just content to hear her calm voice and to feel the strength in those small, slender and utterly competent hands. She would help him to recover. And it would be an ideal opportunity for them to become closer.

The next day he felt a little better and spent more time awake. He had brief visits from Catalina and Fernando, La Quinta's farm manager and his wife, from Carmen, and Isabel—Catalina's young and stunning daughter whom he was putting through horticultural college. They told him that his father was worried but was being kept up to date by frequent bulletins.

Flowers began to arrive. Various friends rang and messages were related to him in such numbers that he became confused. He began to identify Taz's soft, brisk footsteps and enjoyed listening to her speaking to the other four patients in Intensive Care who, like most of the hospital's inmates, were all expats who'd paid into the Laker health insurance scheme for private treatment.

He had to admit that she was a wonderful influence. Instead of a pervading doom and gloom on the ward, which he'd expected, everyone went about their work with a cheerful smile when she was on duty.

Perhaps his estimation of time was hazy, but she seemed to be around a good deal. That night she calmed a petrified mother whose son had crashed his car on the N340 and she sat talking to the woman far into the early hours while they kept vigil by the young man's bed.

He heard the mother wail when her son woke and clearly didn't know her. Jude could tell at once that the young man's brain must have been damaged. The doctors came and spoke in hushed tones to the mother then went away. Taz let the woman cry, holding her supportively without attempting to stop the tears.

And when the sobs became quieter Taz gently told the woman that this was still her son, he was still there as he'd always been, and he needed her more than ever. She spoke comfortingly but never giving false hope and, gradually, Jude felt the strength return to the woman's voice and heard the love in her heart as she talked to her injured son for the first time, offering him comfort and security in the compassionate tone of her voice.

Tears came to Jude's own eyes, his emotions deeply touched. Taz's compassion and understanding amazed him. She offered more than sympathy, he realised, and she gave practical help so that people could deal with situations and feel they were doing some good.

He found this confusing. Her behaviour fitted with the person he'd *thought* she was, when they'd first been together, but not with his subsequent knowledge of her character. Could an amoral, shallow and pleasure-seeking woman really care about the feelings of others?

It didn't make sense. Here, dealing with needy people, she seemed softer, less abrasive. Her face was habitually

sweet and loving and she genuinely seemed to care for those
who were sick and worried.

Perhaps, he mused, she was a natural carer. Some people
needed to have that kind of benign power over others. The
Florence Nightingale syndrome. Well, that was fine. She
could care for him. He'd work on that.

He daydreamed, thinking of her stroking his forehead, the
soft murmur of her voice, the concern and compassion that
flowed from her. In his mind's eye he remembered how she
looked and imagined her dark eyes gazing down on him and
the sweetness of her mouth.

He felt a pain somewhere in his heart. She'd lose interest
in him as soon as he was well. Heaving a sigh, he gave up
trying to evaluate Taz's complex personality. His head
ached.

All he knew was that her administrations went far beyond
the requirements of her job, that she was the most competent
and empathetic nurse on the ward and that, despite all their
differences, he found solace in knowing that she was around.
He smiled, listening to her low, modulated voice nearby, and
fell asleep.

'You must be exhausted, Taz,' said Harvey, meeting her
early the next morning in the deserted staff rest-room. 'You
don't have to work in your leisure time, you know.'

She did. She needed to be there if Jude's condition wors-
ened. 'What else would I do with my time?' she said casually, pouring herself a coffee.

'He...he still won't see Belinda?'

'No. I'm sorry,' she said sadly.

Bel had walked in and there'd been an awful scene. Taz
had been forced to close the ward to visitors because Jude
had been in danger of tearing out his drip and leaping out
of bed in agitation.

'He's going to be all right?'

She pushed back a wayward hank of hair, which had es-
caped from her neat chignon. 'I think so. He's made re-

markable progress. He's young and fit and should recover very well,' she said wearily.

She knew it wasn't an ordinary tiredness. She'd always been strong, with enormous stamina. This exhaustion was emotional. Her nerves had been strung taut ever since he'd been wheeled in.

'Great. That's excellent news!'

'You're a good man to feel sympathy for the guy who's engaged to the woman you love,' Taz said in admiration.

He went pink. 'I wouldn't have wished this on anyone. And I want him to be well for Bel's sake.'

'That's true love,' she said softly, 'to want someone else's happiness above your own. Well, we're moving him to High Dependency, which is progress. I'll continue to keep an eye on him, though.'

'He's important to us.'

Tired as she was, she looked up quickly, alerted by the anxiety in Harvey's voice. 'That's an odd thing to say.'

He hesitated. 'I admire you and so I want to be honest with you, Taz. My interest in Jude's health isn't entirely due to the goodness of my heart. I have to tell you this because Bel's going mad with worry and we need your help. There isn't any easy way to say this, I'm afraid. The hospital's in financial trouble. Your father borrowed heavily to top up his initial investment and he spent money like water on equipment we couldn't afford. He hired some of the best surgeons in a bid to win investors and patronage and...well, I have to admit, Belinda's been taking a large salary and doing nothing in return.'

'But my father was a wealthy man!' she cried in astonishment.

'Not really. He lived on credit and bravado.'

Taz felt the blood drain from her face. A tiny doubt about her father crept into her mind before she firmly erased it. 'Surely not!' she declared.

'Believe me, I managed his finances and I know the sit-

uation better than anyone,' said Harvey. 'There is no money,
Taz. It was exhausted long ago.' He grimaced. 'Your father
could sell snow to polar bears. He lived life on the edge,
and now the edge has fallen away. He could see trouble
coming and I think the strain of pretending to be rich and
hustling for money—plus the champagne and rich food—
finally killed him.'

She stared at Harvey with wide eyes. A terrible sick feeling lurked in her stomach at the idea that her father could
have been a con man as Jude had claimed. And for Harvey
to call her father a hustler—Harvey, who was her father's
right-hand man—was a frightening indictment.

'Someone...' She gulped. 'Someone said he—he was a
crook,' she said huskily.

Harvey avoided her gaze and she felt her pulses racing.
'Taz, we must deal with the present,' he insisted. 'The plain
fact of the matter is that we need Jude to be fit and well
because the Laker Foundation is deeply in debt. Bluntly, we
desperately need his money, his patronage and his manage-
ment flair. Everything he touches does well, you see. His
reputation alone guarantees funds and ensures business. He's
potentially our golden egg. With him, we can't fail. Without
him we go under.'

'Jude?' She frowned. 'But how can that be? Surely his
father's dreadful behaviour ruined his chances of being
trusted—especially by the business community?'

Harvey looked uncomfortable. 'Jude has an unquestioned
standing in the business world. He's built up a huge horticultural business from nothing.'

'A what?' She couldn't believe it. 'He was studying law!
What does he know about plants?'

And then she remembered his love of the land, how he'd
talked of a valley he knew where butterflies drifted in clouds
over aromatic herbs, the sun shining on their iridescent
wings. 'More beautiful than the costliest jewels,' he'd said
softly, and she'd fallen in love with him then.

She smiled, and then recalled how he'd dead-headed a hibiscus in the atrium where they met... And the exotic flowers in Belinda's flat. Horticulture. How astonishing. It gave a different slant on him.

Harvey was saying something and shrugging. 'All I do know is that he's known to be fair and straight and he has won back the respect of the business sector here.'

She struggled to understand this. 'And you're saying that's why you need...'

The penny dropped. She put down her cup carefully and looked Harvey straight in the eyes.

'Does Belinda love him or not?'

Harvey heaved a huge sigh. 'Not.'

She felt a sudden contraction of her lungs. There had been a conspiracy. She'd been duped by her own stepmother. She owed him an apology.

All that chatter from Belinda about adoring Jude had been an act. No wonder she'd sounded odd, sometimes gushing, and sometimes almost guilty. Taz felt she'd been betrayed by people she'd trusted. They'd been lying to her all along.

Once again her judgement had been flawed. Perhaps she should be more wary in future and not make allowances for people. She bit her lip. Like most people, Bel had acted in her own best interests. Maybe, Taz thought, that was something she should always remember.

Harvey adored Bel and the hospital was his baby. So he'd been prepared to protect both, by fair means or foul.

It seemed she could trust no one.

'The marriage is a cold-blooded arrangement on both sides, then,' she said bitterly. And she'd been castigating herself unmercifully because she'd allowed Jude to seduce her!

Harvey nodded guiltily. 'Bel was scared when she learned she'd inherited huge debts. She's got this thing about not having money because of the nightmare experiences she had in her past. It makes her physically sick and she'll do anything to make herself feel rock-solid secure.'

Taz knew how petrified her stepmother was of being poor and hungry again. That didn't excuse her, though. 'And you?' she asked angrily. 'You loved her! How could you bear to let this happen?'

'She and I would have been together even though she was married—'

Taz's gasp of horror cut him short. 'Are you telling me that you would have been *lovers*? How could you do this? It's shocking!'

'I had no choice! I'd do anything for her. I want her to be happy—'

'You'd sacrifice your right to be her husband?' Taz asked in amazement.

'It's what she wanted. She thought she could have everything: money, position, and me. Jude doesn't love her. It wouldn't have hurt him.'

'How long have you been lovers?' she asked in a dangerously quiet voice.

'I comforted her when David died,' he said. 'We fell in love. I told her I couldn't give her the kind of life she'd been used to and told her about the problems with the hospital. She cried. She'd imagined she'd be rich. Taz, you must understand,' he went on, his face alight with passion. 'The hospital is part of my life. I've been here ever since it opened in one job or another. I care about it. The staff, the cleaners, suppliers...I know them all and how much they need us to succeed and keep open. Ten per cent of our patients were charity cases but we've had to stop all non-paying admissions. I hate that!' he said vehemently. 'Think what a disaster it would be if the hospital closes with a mountain of debts!'

She was silent, imagining the effect on the people who worked so hard here. Maria, who brought round the morning and afternoon refreshments, would be out of work and, at sixty, it was doubtful she'd get another job. Carlos the porter wouldn't find employment either, not with his asthma.

And they weren't the only ones who'd suffer. Harvey had somehow acquired several deserving cases on the staff who worked hard and well because he was such a kind and thoughtful boss, but who would struggle to get jobs elsewhere.

When she'd teased him about his generosity once, he'd looked uncomfortable and said that he'd done something in his past that he regretted, and it was his way of making amends.

Passion and fear drove people to do amazing things, she mused. Jude would have married Bel—who'd been prepared to marry Jude. Harvey would have let her.

'Well, I think you've probably only postponed the closure,' she observed quietly. 'Jude still refuses to see Belinda. The engagement's almost certainly off. I think she's all yours, Harvey.'

His shoulders slumped. 'I don't know whether to laugh or cry,' he muttered.

'Why don't you just love her?' she suggested. 'She'll find out what real security can be like if you care deeply about her.'

'And the hospital?' he asked heavily.

She thought how ironic it was that Jude had been on the brink of surrendering his freedom for a pile of debts.

'Jude will have to know the true situation.' She paused, thinking about what had once been unthinkable: working with Jude. But she thought differently now and the situation was desperate. 'Harvey, just one more question—if my father was a crook, does that suggest that maybe Jude's father was telling the truth in court—that he did invest in the hospital? Maybe my father lied...?'

Somehow Harvey stumbled and dropped the pile of papers he was carrying. He bent down to retrieve them and it was a few moments before he rose again looking rather red in the face.

'My father...' Taz reminded him, eager to hear his answer.

Harvey hesitated a moment. 'I don't think your father lied. It would have been difficult to hide that sum of money. And—and I would have known if he had tried...'

Maybe both Mateo and her father were dishonest in their own ways, Taz thought to herself. But the hospital must be saved. 'Perhaps I can persuade Jude to become a partner. It would solve all our problems, Harvey.'

'Could you?' he asked eagerly. 'Would you stick with him and broach the subject as soon as he's better?'

Her heart gave a little jerk. It would mean keeping in touch with Jude instead of watching him walk out of her life for ever. She checked the spurt of pleasure that gave her, knowing that she was grabbing at any excuse to be near him. Was that self-torture or what?

'Leave him to me,' she said firmly. 'Go on. Time you weren't here. Find Bel, tell her you love her and hold her close. That's what she needs, far more than money and material goods—even if she doesn't know it.'

Harvey thanked her and hurried away eagerly. Taz sat in the deserted room, her mind in turmoil. Everything had been turned on its head. Good, kind, honest Harvey had proved to be nothing of the kind. And yet it wasn't that simple. He'd been trying to please Bel and had done his best to keep the hospital afloat. A worthy reason, despite the unworthy solution. And he'd been trying to protect the woman he loved from bankruptcy.

Bel...well, she couldn't entirely blame her. Bel had always been weak and in need of someone else to run her life. She'd had such a terrible childhood that the scars of insecurity would always be with her.

Taz sighed and stretched, aware that she'd learned a great deal about human nature over the past few hours.

And what about Jude? It was pretty certain that he would accept her suggestion of a directorship with alacrity. He'd then be free to marry for love.

She flinched, imagining him with a wife and a cluster of adoring children. With his inevitable involvement in the hospital they'd be seeing a lot of one another. That would be unbearable.

Miserably she picked up her coffee mug, dropped it, and was reminded all over again of the time when Bel had first called to tell her about her new 'lover' and she'd flung coffee in all directions as a result.

'Oh, Bel!' she sighed in exasperation.

Taz rose and mopped up the mess, then carefully washed the mug, only chipping it once. I want him, she thought bleakly. And I don't want any other woman to have him.

Common sense prevailed. In his opinion she had no breeding and wasn't therefore bride material. He'd find a classy Spanish heiress—perhaps one of those women who'd been visiting him...like that gorgeous Isabel. And he'd settle down to make babies in the sure knowledge that their genetic make-up would include pure aristocratic blood and impeccable ancestry.

But at least he was alive, she thought soberly. He could well be dead. Anything was better than that. And, for a while, she would be with him. It was something to enjoy for as long as it lasted.

CHAPTER SEVEN

TAZ returned to the ward, checking her patients, but putting off the moment when she faced Jude.

She felt guilty knowing about Bel and Harvey's scam. Somehow he had to be told—but how? He might dream up some terrible revenge and decide not to help with the hospital's finances. In an agony of indecision, she prolonged her duties, resolutely keeping her back to Jude's bed.

But she was intensely aware of him. He was lying there, racked with pain, the unwitting subject of a calculated deception. Far from exerting his influence over a weak and fragile woman, he'd been cold-bloodedly tricked into an agreement—and would have ended up as a cuckolded husband.

Jude, however, had acted quite openly by making it clear that he didn't love Bel. Looking at the facts dispassionately, all he'd been guilty of in this matter was an excessive loyalty to his father. There was even something to be admired in that.

Goodness and evil weren't as clear-cut as she'd once imagined.

Suddenly she was alerted by the sound that indicated his oxygen mask had slipped. Quickly she hurried over and eased it over his bruised face.

'Taz,' he murmured.

He fumbled for her hand and caught hold of it. A strange sensation of weakness robbed her of her strength and she found herself sitting down beside him, her legs shaking and her breath almost non-existent because of the rapid beating of her heart.

'I'm here,' she whispered.

'I thought that would bring you running,' he said softly.

'You fraud!'

Her indignant but amused smile faded to bitterness. Fraud had been his specialisation. She wished it were otherwise. Was everyone corrupt in one way or another in their efforts to reach their goals in life?

She looked at him and was immediately beguiled by his gentle smile. He seemed so innocent, so happy. And yet he couldn't be. He must be in great pain. So much for outward appearances.

She felt she'd never believe anyone ever again. Her mouth drooped.

'You were spending too long with everyone else. I wanted you,' he said huskily. 'I missed you, Taz.'

'Jude—' she croaked.

'Don't say anything. Just be here.'

She would stay with him for ever if he asked just at this moment. 'I—I'll check your reflexes,' she said hoarsely, grabbing his other hand.

His grip tightened and then relaxed. Satisfied, she transferred her attentions to his feet and legs and then ran through the standard acuity questions breathily. He seemed just as tense as she was, answering in a gravelly whisper that vibrated through her body.

'Very good. Everything's in working order.'

'Certainly is,' he muttered.

She swallowed, hoping he didn't mean what she thought he meant. 'Any pain?' she asked in an unnaturally high voice.

'Everywhere. Can you massage my legs, Nurse?'

She glanced at him suspiciously, but his face was twisted with discomfort. Immediately contrite, she tried to put aside her skittering emotions and briskly peeled back the sheet to reveal one bare leg.

'Is it a cramping pain?' she asked, keeping calm despite her fear that he'd developed an embolism.

'No. Just a general ache from lying here doing nothing.'

'It must be very frustrating.'

'You can say that again.'

Taz went pink. 'I'll get the physio in.'

'No—it'll be hours before she arrives. Help me now.'

Trying desperately to blank out her mind, she worked to release the tautness. And beneath her hands the muscle fibres lengthened and relaxed.

'To the left. Up a bit. Perfect,' he purred.

'You sound a lot better,' she observed drily.

'I'm tough. A survivor. I've had to be over the years,' he replied.

She felt a flash of sympathy. 'Was it hard when your father lost his influence with the business community?' she asked.

'It was hell.' He clenched his jaw and winced from the pain. 'I don't want to think of it, Taz. I want to forget. The present is more important now. And the future. I want you to know something.'

With brisk efficiency she tucked the sheets around his legs again. 'Go on.'

'I don't want you to think I'm ratting on your stepmother,' he said carefully, 'but you must know how—and why—the accident happened.'

'If you feel up to it—'

'There's nothing wrong with my mouth or my voice. And my head's clearer now. I want the record to be set straight.' He paused and then went on, 'Quite simply, I told Belinda that I wasn't going to marry her.'

Taz stared. 'Why?' she asked cautiously.

'She's Harvey's lover,' he said bluntly. 'I'm not into sharing.'

So he knew. Harvey hadn't told her that! Probably his mind was too full of his own problems.

'I let her keep the ring,' he added, his mouth wry. 'But I

think she flipped because I asked her to hand over the platinum credit card.'

Taz winced, but could well believe it. 'What makes you think she and Harvey are lovers?' she asked.

'I went round to his flat and found she'd spent the night there. I won't bore you with the details.'

'Oh. How awful,' she whispered, imagining the blow to his pride. 'Jude...I knew. Harvey spoke to me about this half an hour ago—'

'Would you have told me?' He shot the words at her.

She sighed. 'Oh, yes! I don't know how or when, but I couldn't have let you continue in ignorance. Perhaps when you were a little better. I'm sorry, Jude. But at least you found out in time. They're very much in love.'

Jude's face was grim. 'That doesn't excuse what they planned.'

'No. I'm ashamed of them both. I actually saw you arguing with her in the street,' she said hesitantly.

'Not arguing. I was telling her she was destroying herself. She was drunk again. I imagine she was finding the deception harder and harder to maintain. One man for love, one for money. Running two at once must have been a strain,' he added bitterly.

'Drunk? At ten in the morning?' Taz cried in disbelief.

His lip curled in weary contempt. 'Why should I lie? Think about it. You must know she's an alcoholic. Surely you have noticed how rapidly her moods alter, depending on whether she's been drinking or not? And you can't have missed the smell of alcohol when we walked into the flat.'

So that was what it had been. She thought of Belinda's manic behaviour, how she used to be edgy and jittery, then disappear—and then, just as suddenly, she'd be in a party mood. She remembered the bottle, which had been hidden behind the cushions, and Jude's displeasure.

'I'm hopeless,' she said dispiritedly. 'I never realised.'

'Don't be hard on yourself. With an addiction like that people become adept at disguising their condition.'

'Was she drunk the night I arrived?' she asked quietly.

'Yes. She was worried that you'd find out what she was up to—and that you'd discover her craving for alcohol.'

'So you stalled me to protect her.'

He gave a small shrug. 'That's right. She thinks she needs alcohol because she feels inadequate socially. And lately she must have been very unhappy.'

'I know. But...she put herself in that situation. I'm so sorry, Jude.'

'No one likes being made a fool of,' he said softly.

'No.' He was justly annoyed. Knowing him, he might even decide to take some kind of revenge. 'Jude,' she said urgently, 'don't be hard on her. You know how fragile she is.'

His breathing sounded laboured. 'My guess is that she's as tough as an ox,' he muttered. 'But don't worry. It's an episode in my life I want to draw a veil over.' And he sounded tired when he said, 'She deceived us both, Taz.'

'I know,' she said miserably. 'I wish I'd believed you when you said she didn't love you. I was wrong. I trusted the wrong person. Forgive me.'

'It's over. I'm well out of it. I hope to change your suspicions about me some day. I'm not evil, Taz.'

Her eyes shimmered with tears. 'I know that,' she said jerkily. 'I've discovered that no one's entirely good or bad. People act for their own survival—'

'Or for those they love,' he amended.

He was referring to what he'd been prepared to do for his father six years ago. But in her book seducing a virgin for monetary gain was still reprehensible.

'I must go,' she said croakily. 'I'll see you in the morning.'

'Talk to me during your break tomorrow,' he pleaded. 'I

want to know all about you, what you've been doing these past six years.'

She hesitated, but was so anxious to get away that she nodded her head and hurried away. Whatever she felt for him, she must remember his basic character. He used people for his own ends and had no respect for her. She must be careful and guard her emotions or she'd get hurt.

But when she called in to see how he was the next day he'd been moved to a private room—a good sign—and his eagerness and beaming smile won her over. Taz was so delighted to see him sitting in an armchair and looking less wan and tired that she smiled back, her pleasure lighting her eyes.

'I've been waiting for hours!' he declared, slipping off his headphones and patting the chair beside him. 'I'm so bored I've been reduced to singing along with the hospital radio! I hold you to your promise. Entertain me!' he said with an appealing, lopsided grin.

'You're selfish and demanding,' she scolded.

'I'm supposed to be. It's my role. I'm a patient.'

Taz sat down and flung him a scathing look. 'Patient doesn't come into it.'

He laughed. 'Indulge me. I might even fall asleep and you can tiptoe away and annoy someone else by reprimanding them.' He took her hand in his. 'So you don't escape,' he said softly.

It was the last thing on her mind. She gazed at him, her heart turning over with… She closed her eyes as the truth hit her between the eyes. With a greater love than she could have believed possible.

'Are you talking? Have I gone deaf?' he complained, cupping his ear.

'I'm thinking,' she croaked.

'Slow process, isn't it?' he murmured, his eyes dancing.

'Yes.'

It had taken her all this time to realise that her feelings

for him were very different. She thought of the desperate urgency of her love when they'd been younger and how that had changed. This was deeper, almost serene in its certainty. If the accident hadn't occurred she would never have known that she'd never stopped loving him, or that her hatred had been her way of coping with that fact.

She realised that her love for Jude was more profound than she'd ever imagined. His actions had been wrong and, for a while, she had lost respect for him. Following Bel and Harvey's revelations, she understood a little more how people could truly believe that they were doing the right thing.

Perhaps she was too ready to excuse people, Jude in particular. But she knew how much he loved his father, and how hard it must have been for Jude to admit that his father had lied to him about the investment.

And so her love was intact. It felt deeper and rock-solid. A wistful smile softened the seriousness of her face.

'Taz!'

She jumped. 'What?'

'I've got a hot date in three weeks,' he said, pretending to look at a non-existent watch. 'Any chance of a chat before then?'

'You're far too perky,' she reproved, loving his banter. 'I'll have to dose you with something nasty.'

'Cut out the S and M and just talk, will you?' he said, pretending exasperation.

Taz giggled and surrendered, feeling she was falling down a very slippery slope indeed. But she adored being with him, ached to hurry back to him whenever she was away, and had spent the whole of the previous night thinking of him. Love unrequited, she thought with a sigh.

'This week? Before my hair grows to my waist?' Jude said hopefully, running a hand over his close-cropped scalp.

'I'm gathering my thoughts,' she said with dignity.

'Rely on instinct,' he said huskily. 'Live dangerously.'

He held her gaze for a long time and she felt herself weakening fatally.

'Right,' she said, clearing her clogged throat. 'Here we go.'

Taz made the events of the past six years of her life as amusing as possible. You couldn't get moony and sentimental when you were laughing. She picked key events and made them entertaining.

'So I was absolutely creased up with nerves and somehow, I don't know how, I threw the hot tea all over the front of the head of nursing's Armani suit.'

'And you kissed goodbye to the dream job in Madrid,' Jude said, his amusement turning to sympathy.

'Oh, no!' she exclaimed. 'He stripped off his jacket and shirt while I sat there glued to my seat, wondering if he was preparing some awful punishment. He calmly sent out for some calamine, then asked if I'd like a refill and was it one or two sugars?'

Jude's rich laughter rang out and she felt delirious with happiness. He seemed so much better. It didn't matter what happened to him when he left hospital. If he married, then she hoped he'd be happy. All she wanted was his full recovery and she couldn't ask for more.

'You're a dangerous woman where stimulants are involved,' he observed drily.

She gave him a suspicious look but he seemed innocent enough. 'No. Just clumsy,' she sighed. And then she quickly drew her hand from his when there was a knock on the door. 'You have a visitor,' she said brightly. She smiled at Isabel whose beautiful face was just visible above a huge basket of fruit.

'Isabel!' he cried, pleasure warming his voice.

And, as she left Jude's bedside, Taz realised that he must have identified the young woman by scent alone.

Upset by the implications of that, she went back to work. Later, when she read to Jude during her lunch hour, she wondered how many women he knew intimately enough to know their individual perfumes.

By the end of the week he was fretting to be well again. He was never ill. Feeling like this, initially so helpless and dependent on others, had given him a deeper insight into his father's plight. His thoughts on this hadn't been easy to bear. Jude wished there was more he could do other than show his love and devotion.

What must it be like, he wondered, to know you would never recover, never enjoy walking in the sun over your own land, chatting to friends and having the freedom of independence? What a hell of a life. Undeserved, unavenged.

He frowned, painfully aware that there was one thing his father wanted in life—and therefore it was up to him to make sure he had it. Time was running out. Jude pressed a hand against his head where the pain raged and knew he wasn't well enough to seduce Taz. Unless he appealed to that Nightingale spirit.

She'd continued to visit him in her spare time and, despite his many other visitors, he particularly looked forward to her arrival and the sound of her low, liquid voice as she brought the events in the daily paper to life. Listening to her read was so enjoyable that he'd neglected to tell her that his sight was virtually normal again.

She sat now in the chair beside his bed, giggling as she recounted some silly item about a man whose dog wouldn't let his new bride sleep in the marital bed. As she related the odd story, assuming different voices for the defensive husband and irritated bride, he was able to indulge himself and watch her almost unobserved.

Thick and luxurious lashes veiled the rich brown eyes that would meet his in a moment and be sparkling with laughter. Her soft mouth framed the strong white teeth as she read and a glow of colour highlighted her strong cheekbones.

He clasped his hands together because he wanted to pull

her to him, stroke her sweet face, take that cute earlobe between his lips and inhale all her life and vigour.

But, above all, he felt a wonderful sensation of peace whenever she was with him. It was probably something to do with the patient-nurse effect. Now he understood why patients fell for nurses or doctors. It was a time of extreme vulnerability and a strange intimacy and he'd become infatuated with an image of a perfect woman—even though he knew that image to be flawed.

Taz enjoyed sex. Fine by him, but she didn't care who contributed to that enjoyment. It would be disastrous for him to overlook that fact and he had to make sure his lust didn't turn his brain.

'I'm discharging myself today,' he said casually, when she paused to turn the page.

Her dismay stupidly flattered his ego. 'You're not well enough!' she protested, and he wryly reminded himself that she was speaking professionally, not wistfully yearning for him to stay and clutter up the ward.

'I'm worried about my father,' he said quietly. 'I've decided I must go for his sake. He's not well, Taz.'

'Neither are you!' she cried, leaning forward anxiously.

A sharp pang seared through his chest because she seemed genuinely concerned. She was a nurse, he told himself sternly. Of course she was interested in his welfare.

He shrugged. 'I might as well lie around at home, as here.'

And he thought of having her at La Quinta, all to himself, instead of sharing her with other patients. His heart began to pound and a heat swept through his body.

'Look at you! You're flushed, even now!' Her eyes were accusing as she picked up his hand and took his pulse. 'As I thought! Racing like a Formula One car!'

'I wish I had that much throttle,' he observed drily.

She put her hand on his forehead and he breathed in her warmth, lifting his face so that he could feel the faint whisper of her breath on his skin. It did the most extraordinary things to his lungs.

'Open!' she commanded, popping a thermometer into his obedient mouth. 'You mustn't go, Jude,' she pleaded, her crisply covered breasts far too close for his heart rate to settle. It revved up strongly enough to overtake a racing driver.

God. He was fantasising. Doctors and nurses. He couldn't wait.

'It's madness!' she said, noting his bright eyes. 'You could have a fever. You need nursing—'

'I know. But I'm going and you can't stop me,' he mumbled around the thermometer.

'This is stupid!' she said crossly. 'If your father knew how ill you are he'd tell you to stay put.'

'I'm not ill. Just hot. Anyway, there's a car coming for me at three o'clock.'

'I don't believe this! You—you could have a relapse,' she said in a panic-stricken voice. 'A clot on the lungs. Reaction to the drugs...anything.'

He was intrigued by her anxiety to keep him there. To his surprise she whipped out the thermometer far too soon and stared at it, frowning, her lips pursed. He thought of kissing them and shifted uncomfortably in case she saw where his imagination had taken him.

'I don't think it was in long enough,' he said helpfully.

Taz stared at him blankly, dropped the thermometer to the floor and jumped back from it, quite bewildered.

'I've never done that before!' she cried in agitation.

'I think it's a hint that you need a break too. You've been working too hard,' Jude told her soothingly.

Her startled eyes flicked to meet his watchful gaze. He was going and she couldn't do anything to stop him. This could be the last time she saw him unless she could come up with an excuse to visit him at home. She was anxious about the future of the hospital, of course.

And pigs might fly, she told herself. That wasn't the main reason. Conscious of a growing sense of emptiness, she stood looking at him for a long, wistful moment, greedily taking in every detail, seeing beyond the bruised face to the man she loved beneath.

Miserably she picked up the undamaged thermometer and thrust it in the bin, accepting her fate but unable to hide her sadness. If she didn't do something to stop him then Jude would go, the hospital would fail and everyone here would be looking for work. Bel included.

He would leave her life. She dragged in a rasping breath. 'I'll get your discharge form,' she said listlessly.

'You could nurse me at home,' Jude murmured.

Her head snapped up, a brief hope illuminating her face. It was just as quickly dashed. How could she combine her shifts here with caring for him?

'It's impossible, Jude,' she said, feeling desperately low-spirited.

'The invitation's open to Graham too.'

She wasn't to be amused. 'I can hardly leave my job just because you want me to.' Not that there'd be a job for her to stay in after a couple of months or so, she thought gloomily.

'Look at me, Taz.' Jude's eyes seemed to bore right into her head. 'I want you to ask Harvey to release you for a short while,' he said quietly. 'He owes me a favour, don't you think? I will pay you ten per cent over your present salary to compensate for any inconvenience; all board and lodging will be included. And I'll stand the cost of a re-placement nurse here—'

'Why?' she jerked out in curiosity. And cursed herself because it was a wonderful idea and she didn't want it to fail—though fail it must.

'You're the best,' he said simply. 'And I've become used to having only the best.'

There was a silence. She could hear him breathing heavily

and realised he wasn't as fit as he made out. He needed someone to nurse him—why *should* it be someone else? She knew him, knew the small signs of tiredness, the way he hid his pain, stoically withstood his headaches without demanding relief, and she recognised those odd moments when his heart raced and he needed soothing. No one would do the job better.

Harvey would almost certainly agree to the proposition. He'd be overjoyed because she could use her time profitably to persuade Jude to help save the hospital. And yet she was needed on the ICU ward. She bit her lip, wishing she could be in two places at once.

'I—I don't know,' she stammered.

'I need to be at home for my father's sake,' he explained. 'You'll understand when you meet him.'

'I—I'd like to meet him, too,' she said hesitantly. It was a golden opportunity, but...

'That's settled, then.'

Excitement fizzed like a heady wine to her head and she couldn't stop smiling. She'd be abandoning her current patients but there would be a tremendous gain in the long run—Harvey would be sure to see that.

And the team on ICU had taken on some of her ideas and the ward worked like clockwork—well, a machine with a human face and heart, she amended, remembering with pleasure the friendly atmosphere that now prevailed.

Taz felt a blush of colour surge to her cheeks. She could rationalise her reasons for agreeing to Jude's suggestion as much as she liked, but she knew why she was so keen.

'I'll do what I can,' she said, desperately anxious to know Harvey's decision. 'But I can't promise.'

'I categorically refuse to be nursed by anyone else but you,' he said firmly.

'I thought I was the wicked witch?' she demurred.

'You are. But your jokes are better than anyone else's. And you know I need you,' he said in a low voice.

She quivered and was bewildered by the happiness that simple but sincere remark had given her. Here we go again, she thought, despairing of her common sense.

'You and all my other patients,' she said lightly.

'But you're not emotionally tied to them.'

They exchanged a long and searching look. 'I suppose exasperation counts as an emotion,' she fielded, feeling her heartbeat increasing.

He gave a faint smile. 'It'll do.'

'It'll have to. I'll go and see Harvey now.'

'Taz.'

She shook at the intensity of feeling in his voice. 'Uh-huh?' she said casually, not turning to face him.

'If he says no, I'll abduct you. And that's not an empty threat.'

'You and whose army?' she scoffed and hurried away, her footsteps light, her heart racing with joy.

She wanted this very much, however unwise it might be for her personally. She could see that she might be hurt. But it would be worth it if she could be with him a little longer. The hospital would be saved.

Later that afternoon she and Jude were comfortably ensconced in the back of his chauffeur-driven car and travelling along the Ronda road to La Quinta.

In a haze of delight Taz gazed at the scenery, the car windows wide open so that Jude could smell and hear the scents and sounds of the countryside he loved so much.

As she'd thought, Harvey had jumped at the chance for her to spend time with Jude. He'd brushed aside her hesitant protest that she really ought to remain at the hospital, and had said that it was running on a tightrope and the rope was sagging badly, so her efforts were far more important elsewhere.

He'd looked tired and harassed. Usually his hair was neat and tidy but he'd evidently thrust his hands through it so many times in despair that it had been a mess. Papers had littered the desk and the phone had rung continually, the calls being mainly from irate suppliers, judging by Harvey's reaction.

Cigarette butts had filled the ashtray in front of him as he'd chain-smoked and had apologised for doing so, saying that he'd taken up smoking again to soothe his nerves.

Harvey's desperation had brought the situation home to her. He'd told her that the staff were complaining because supplies were being held up and they were short of essentials. Short cuts were being taken. The possibility of a disaster loomed every day.

Taz had listened in horror. She'd learned that the reason was that the hospital's credit had run out. It was on the brink of closure.

Her mind had reeled with the implications of moving the seriously ill patients to other hospitals. People's lives would be put in danger. It didn't bear thinking about. Something had to be done.

She pictured herself, Bel and Harvey facing the staff and telling them that their wages couldn't be paid because the hospital was bankrupt. It would be a terrible end to her father's dream. She dreaded that moment and would do anything to avoid it and the terrible risk in transferring sick patients.

She was convinced. And now her one hope was Jude. Very soon, when he was well enough for a frank discussion, he would grab the chance to buy into a directorship. And then all their troubles would be over.

Taz felt both exhilarated and apprehensive about the future. Could she stay near Jude and not reveal her feelings for him?

And then she smiled, entranced despite her worries. The road was winding above the silver ribbon of a river. The smell of cistus and the sound of goats' bells were pouring through the window. She looked out at the elms and cypresses on the hills and the snowy mountains beyond.

'I love it out here,' she said softly. 'My favourite kind of place. Jude, I think we should stop for a while. You've been sitting for too long and you ought to move about a bit.'

'Yes, Nurse,' he said demurely, but she thought there was a teasing sparkle in his eyes. He spoke to the driver and soon they pulled up by a farm track.

'I wish you could see everything clearly,' she said with a sigh as she guided him to the gate.

'I... Describe it,' he muttered.

'Oh...the sky is an intense blue. Cloudless,' she said, keeping her arm tucked in his. 'You can feel the heat. Can you smell the earth? The wild lavender and thyme—oh, and clary—are being invaded by butterflies...and there's a field below of wheat and poppies. It's glorious.'

'And there's a black kite overhead.'

'How did you know?' she asked in astonishment.

He grinned. 'There always is!' His head lifted. 'I can smell rosemary, too. Tilled land somewhere—'

'Yes, beneath the olive grove! Your senses are very keen. They haven't been affected by your broken nose.'

'My senses are telling me that you're wearing...' he leaned lightly against her '...a very light fragrance. So light it's probably just soap. Jasmine,' he said triumphantly, his face very close to hers.

'Right,' she said shakily.

The skirt of her blue dress fluttered in the breeze. Jude had insisted that she did not wear her uniform, saying he'd feel too much like an invalid if she did. But now, as he cocked his head to one side in a listening attitude and caught the fabric in his hand, feeling its texture with his fingers, she wished she was in something more formal and protective. Like a suit of armour.

'Cotton. What colour?' he asked innocently.

'Blue. Jude—'

'Blue.' His hands came to rest on her hips. 'Fitted. What kind of neckline?'

She pulled away. It was either that, or risk his exploratory fingers around the deep V of the dress. 'It's not important!' she cried hotly. 'Is your eyesight really that poor?'

'Humour me. I like to visualise people about me,' he explained.

Taz wondered if he'd asked Isabel the same questions. And if she'd allowed him to discover what kind of neckline she had. Taz gave a silent groan. This tearing jealousy was destructive. If he fancied Isabel she could hardly blame him.

'Shall we walk along the track a little way to pump the oxygen around my body? I'll need my guide dog handy for safety,' he said companionably, drawing her close again.

There was far too much oxygen in hers. Her lungs were tight and full and her head buzzed as if she'd inhaled a magnum of champagne. Guide dog indeed! She had a suspicion that he was playing a game of some sort with her. Or he just liked women's company, she thought gloomily. Some men had to have a female on their arm or in their beds.

'Just a short distance,' she cautioned sullenly.

'Yes, Nurse,' he agreed, all meek and mild.

She gave him a scathing glance. 'Don't push your luck, Jude.' Feeling flattened by his automatic flirting, she opened the gate. 'I'm supposed to be looking after you so don't make fun of me or I'll *really* get into the bossy matron routine—'

'Dominatrix,' he murmured dreamily and then laughed. 'Don't worry! My tastes are normal.'

'How did you know I was worried?' she challenged.

'Your body stiffened up. I've become super-sensitive to it lately,' he murmured. Taz blushed and hoped he couldn't sense that too. 'I do need your guidance, Taz. Please?'

'I'd be failing in my duties if I let you fall over the edge of the path and into the valley below,' she grudgingly conceded.

He offered his elbow and she slipped her arm into it.

Together they walked down the path and Taz allowed the warm, drowsy air to soothe her irritation.

She'd known what he was like. She'd walked into this with her eyes wide open.

Small white houses topped with hooped tiles, typical of the famous White Villages of Andalusia, scrambled down a distant hill. The ruins of a Moorish castle topped a crag, dominating the skyline. The path offered stunning views of the silt-laden river winding in the valley below and, as Taz began to describe this to Jude, she felt herself soften and relax.

'There's a little farm ahead,' she said, charmed by the scene. 'Tiny. Vines and roses over the door and onions drying on the earth. A mule in the yard beneath a juniper.'

'Birdsong in the air, an irrigation channel nearby—if I'm not mistaken—and a beautiful woman by my side. What more could a man want?' he murmured.

'A cup of coffee and a doughnut if you're anything like me,' she said practically, desperate to break the romantic mood. Her chest was beginning to hurt from the poignancy of it all. 'Come on. That's enough walking. Back to the car. And don't say "Yes, Nurse"!'

'No, Nurse,' he said obediently and they both laughed.

His arm came around her waist and she didn't push it away. The moment was too precious and the pressure of his hand too welcome.

He could have died, she said to herself soberly. And here he was, alive, beside her...laughing and teasing her just like the old times. It was too good to be true.

But she vowed to enjoy every moment and to take life as it came, knocks and all. She sighed in contentment. He stumbled and she reached out to steady him, feeling the taut strength of his stomach muscles beneath her flattened palm.

'Seek not for paradise,' he said in his soft, velvety voice.

'It is here—it is here!' she completed huskily, knowing the old saying.

In the car, he sat close to her and she felt as if the distance between them was as nothing. She was totally aware of each movement he made, every breath he took. They were silent with their own thoughts, but it was an intimate silence and she felt happier than she had for a very long time, her imagination weaving fantasies which she dared not hope might come true.

If only, she thought wistfully. If only.

CHAPTER EIGHT

HER first glimpse of his house took her breath away. Awed, she turned to Jude, who was smiling, his eyes tightly shut and a blissful expression on his face.

'It's stunning,' she breathed. 'I wish you could see it clearly.'

'Oh, I see it very well indeed,' he said huskily. 'It's etched on my mind.'

And she knew it would always be fixed in her memory too. The imposing house, a dazzling white with corn-coloured hoop tiles, had been sited spectacularly against the distant mountain backdrop. The design of its towers hinted of ancient times when the highly civilised and cultured Muslims had loved and ruled Andalusia, leaving a legacy of beautiful buildings and gardens—and from interbreeding they had left a more visceral legacy of intense passions and honour which must be avenged at all costs.

This was Jude's heritage. She must always remember that he was a hedonist, a lover of pleasure, and that his blood ran hot and strong.

She saw more evidence of Moorish influence. In the formal gardens at the front of the house, a long water-channel flanked by lavender bushes led to an ornamental pool with a fountain. And around the wide terrace there was a riot of colour from a tumble of exotic climbing plants, most of which she didn't recognise.

'Tell me what you think,' he said, as if her opinion mattered.

'It's the most beautiful house I've ever seen, Jude,' she said softly.

'La Quinta has been in Corderro hands for centuries,' he

murmured, love lending a glow to his damaged face. 'It's part of me,' he said simply and his voice grew almost hushed. 'I feel as if I've grown from the soil, as if my roots go down deep within the earth. My ancestors lived and loved and died here. It seems to me that I know every blade of grass, each bough of every tree. I could be blindfolded and dropped anywhere and I'd know where I was from the feel of the ground beneath my feet. It's as familiar to me as the back of my own hand and I love it with an overwhelming passion that probably only my father could understand. I want to see my children playing here.' He paused, emotion overtaking him. 'My...children,' he repeated hoarsely, staring into space as if transfixed by the thought of being a father.

Yes, she thought, a shadow dulling the brightness of her eyes. This place would arouse fierce loyalties. He and his father would willingly lie and cheat to keep their beloved land. She shivered, oddly excluded by the intensity of his feelings for La Quinta.

And it drove home to her more forcibly the kind of wife he would choose to bear his children. La Quinta was too important to risk an influx of unsuitable genes. He'd need someone who was used to servants and grand dinner parties and who could organise a charity ball with a glass of fino sherry in one hand and the other tied behind her back.

His wife would need to fit in with the jet set and talk about designer clothes, suggest little shopping trips to Paris and New York and spend her days lounging by pools with a mobile phone ringing with invitations to balls and charity dos.

Taz's father had appeared to have wealth but, as an ex door-to-door salesman, the Spanish aristocracy had never accepted him. Taz grew silent, realising why Jude had never brought her to this house when they'd been together six years ago—and why he hadn't even told her of its existence.

She simply wasn't worthy of the honour and he would have been embarrassed by her gaucheries.

Only now, as a nurse, was she remotely acceptable. And even then she'd be packed off when society came to call, or she'd sit silently in a corner and sew fine seams like Jane Eyre, she thought ruefully.

'Graham's quiet,' Jude murmured.

'He's overwhelmed. He hasn't seen magnolias before,' she retorted with an effort at resurrecting her confidence.

'If he's worried about meeting my father, I can assure you he'll be charmed,' Jude said. 'Father is looking forward to this meeting.'

She doubted that. He was probably appalled that his son was bringing a Laker to his house. 'Fan of giraffes, is he?'

Jude laughed and then his face became guarded. 'When you've unpacked, we'll have tea—just the two of us. There's something I must explain before you meet Father.'

She didn't reply, her nerves so strained she could hardly keep still. Her meeting with Mateo could be crucial. She must persuade him to release Jude from his promise to avenge himself on the Laker family. Only then could she ask Jude to buy into a directorship.

She'd known Mateo before, when she'd visited Jude at the family villa in Puerto Banus. They'd got on well until the tussle over the hospital. Perhaps he was ashamed of his behaviour and wanted to make amends, she thought hopefully.

She wondered if Jude was going to give her a quick course in etiquette. Her knees began to shake, and down by her left foot Graham quivered, his tongue flapping maniacally.

Jude held her hand and grinned at her, but fear had sucked all smiles from her face. She sat bolt upright and looked anxiously ahead, startled when people seemed to stream out from all parts of the grounds to gather by the huge oak door.

'You've got a welcoming committee,' she cried in surprise, immediately struck by the joy on everyone's face.

Jude was loved. Her heart somersaulted. Harvey's description of Jude's fairness came to mind. Maybe Jude could truly be a good man. He must be, if the tears and greetings from these honest workers could be relied on. You couldn't fool people you employed.

'Gently,' she warned the jostling crowd, when Jude emerged from the car. But she needn't have worried. They treated him like cut glass, exclaiming over his bruised face in horror and trying to decide whether they liked his short hairstyle or not.

With tears streaming down her face, a grey-haired woman took his arm and tenderly ushered him inside. Taz remembered that this woman had visited him in hospital where she'd brought Jude a cardigan she'd knitted. It was thick and gaudy, plainly not something he would have chosen, but he'd put it on at once and had hugged the woman affectionately. It had been a touching scene and she'd warmed to his thoughtfulness.

Now she stood surrounded by the little knot of people, listening to their exclamations of sympathy and delight and realising that Jude was a more complex person than she'd originally thought.

A couple she recognised as two more of his frequent visitors, introduced her as his nurse and she was immediately hugged and thanked by everyone. And then there was a touch on her arm and she looked up to see Isabel. Her heart sank to find her there.

'Hello,' Isabel said, with a dazzling warm smile. 'Welcome to La Quinta, Taz. Sorry Jude's been whisked off and you've been abandoned, but I don't think he had much choice. Carmen's been so upset. I think she wants him to herself for a moment. She's known the family for sixty years, so she has certain privileges.'

'I understand,' Taz said readily, envying Isabel's composure.

'I'll show you your room. It's next to Jude's so you can be near him,' said the lovely Isabel, for all the world as if she were the mistress of the house.

'Thank you,' Taz replied, biting back her terrible jealousy.

They crossed the white marble floor of the shady hall and mounted an imposing staircase. There were huge oil paintings around the walls and beautiful antiques everywhere. Jude—or his father—was seriously rich. Ill-gotten gains? she wondered uncomfortably.

'Mr Corderro senior hasn't come to greet his son,' she said suddenly. 'Does he know Jude is home? Jude's been so agitated—'

Isabel stopped at the top of the stairs in front of a high-arched window and stared at Taz. 'Of course he knows. Jude will see him once he's had tea with you,' she said gently. 'First you must settle yourself in and freshen up.'

'I don't want Jude tiring himself out,' Taz said anxiously. 'He shouldn't be out of hospital. He must rest as much as possible—'

Isabel laughed. 'You'll be lucky! I think you're going to have trouble stopping him from going straight back to work!'

'He'll do as I tell him! I'll go into dragon mode,' Taz said darkly and the two women laughed conspiratorially.

She couldn't help but like Isabel. There was something open and trusting about her. As they walked swiftly along carpeted corridors, Taz hoped fervently that this wasn't another woman who'd been dazzled by Jude's charm.

Leaving directions for Taz to find the drawing room, Isabel left Taz to unpack. Quickly she put her clothes away in the big sandalwood wardrobe and, after a quick wash, she unpinned her hair and brushed it hard, twisting it into a simple knot before setting off to find Jude.

But somewhere she made a wrong turning and ended up

in a narrow corridor with an open arch leading into the central courtyard. Wafting on the air was the scent of roses and jasmine and as she passed the archway she heard the sound of Jude's voice.

Stepping out, she found herself immediately drenched in sunlight. There was a wonderfully refreshing sound of splashing from the fountain in the central pool of carp, which was shaded by huge palms.

Beneath a stone pine in one corner of the courtyard were Jude and his father, sitting on a deeply cushioned ottoman. Even at this distance Taz could see the change in Mateo's appearance. He looked very ill indeed.

She could intrude, or slip quietly away. While she hesitated uncertainly, a light gust of wind rustled her skirts against the rough trunk of a palm. Instantly, Jude turned in her direction and, although he couldn't see very well, she knew he would have identified the source of the sound.

'Hello! I've lost my way!' she called out merrily.

'Taz!'

He rose to his feet. His father remained sitting and she hoped it was because of his ill health and not a lack of respect. As she hovered there, fidgeting, she saw that Jude seemed taken aback as if he hadn't bargained on her meeting his father right now.

'I—I'll go back. Find Isabel. The drawing room,' she mumbled incoherently, dismayed by his lack of welcome.

'No. I—' He was clearly disturbed. 'Come on. This is as good an opportunity as any.'

She came forward, her eyes troubled as she glanced at Mateo's stony face, which was twisted in anger or distaste; she wasn't sure which. Her head came up. How dared he treat her like dirt? She was equal to any lying, cheating Corderro!

'This is Taz, Father,' Jude said flatly. 'Remember I said she'd been nursing me?'

Taz smiled coolly and held out her hand but Mateo

Corderro merely winked. Jude shifted uncomfortably. Well, she thought, she had manners, even if Mateo didn't.

'I remember you well,' she said with considerable dignity, as if nothing was the matter. 'We used to play backgammon together and you always let me win.'

She thought there was a ghost of a smile on the oddly lopsided features and frowned, realising something was wrong.

'I'm sure he remembers, Taz,' Jude said quietly, drawing up a wicker chair for her. 'Please sit down. And please bear with his lack of response—'

'I know!' she gasped suddenly, sitting down opposite the two men. All the signs were there. Poor man. Her heart went out to him and she looked Mateo straight in the eye. 'You've had a stroke, haven't you?'

He winked. A flood of emotion welled up inside her and she reached out to enclose his hand in hers. This was why Jude had wanted to talk to her before meeting his father, and why he'd been disconcerted when she'd turned up accidentally.

'Do you understand what I say?' she asked gently. There was another wink. It was all she could do not to let out a sob. She could hardly bear to see him like this. He'd been so handsome, so vigorous and vital. 'Good!' She gave a wicked grin. 'We can have the kind of chat I like, where I do all the talking!'

The faint smile lifted one corner of his mouth. Her questioning eyes went to Jude.

'When did this happen?' she asked croakily.

He hesitated, glanced at his father and then quietly said, 'When the investigators decided that he had no case against your father.'

She flinched, and when she faced Mateo again there were tears in her eyes. 'I'm sorry,' she said softly. 'I really mean that.'

Her brain whirled. Seeing his father struck down so cruelly must have triggered Jude's decision to take drastic steps towards revenge. Now she understood how he'd been driven to extremes.

'I'm sorry for both of you,' she said earnestly, her voice low and sympathetic. 'And it must be so irritating, Mateo, with everyone jumping to conclusions about what you want and think—and getting it wrong half the time.'

The pained eyes twinkled and she gave a weak smile in return. All the while she was thinking that he and Jude would never rest till they'd taken vengeance in one way or another for the terrible consequences of the investigation. Her lower lip trembled. That revenge could be to let the hospital go under. Jude might enjoy dancing on its grave.

'You understand why I was anxious to come home,' Jude said.

'Oh, I do!' She faced Mateo again. 'And you must have been beside yourself with worry about Jude,' she said with compassion. 'But everything's fine. He's doing very well. I'm only here because the surgeons insisted.' She tried to sound cheerful. 'I think my role will be to shout at him a lot and stop him from doing too much,' she added, managing a shaky little grin.

Jude touched his father's hand, almost caressing it, and she felt her heart lurch to see the love between them both. One totally reliant on the other. One stubbornly fighting a battle for the other. It was incredibly sad. Of course Jude had been upset when it had happened. Of course he'd wanted to lash out at the people he thought responsible.

'Father,' he said wryly, 'I have no wish to subject you to the sound of this woman shrieking at me. I think I'd better go to my room before I'm banished there!' He leaned forward in a conspiratorial manner, his mouth quirked into the mischievous smile that Taz adored. 'If I'm very well-behaved, I believe she might let me come down briefly for dinner—'

'No,' she said firmly. 'Before dinner, yes, and no alcohol.

Then you must go back to bed. You've done quite enough for your first day out.'

Jude opened his hands in a gesture of hopeless resignation. 'You see how it is, Father? I'm to be bullied in my own home.'

'It's about time someone took you in charge,' Taz quipped, seeing how much their chatter was amusing Jude's father.

'Here's our tea,' said Jude, sounding relieved. 'Lemon, mint or English?'

It was very peaceful in the courtyard, with only the sounds of the fountain and the cooing doves and the twitter of martins breaking into their quiet conversation.

She explained Jude's treatment and the plans for his recovery to Mateo and he sat silently, watching her. To save Jude from the effort, she helped Mateo to drink and to eat some sweet pastries and cake. Then she sent Jude off to his room for a rest.

Mateo was clearly enjoying her bossiness. Seeing a book beside him, she hesitantly asked if he'd like her to read for a while. And when he winked she picked up the book of poems and lost herself in the beauty of the words.

Jude watched her from his room, that dark head gleaming in the bright sun, her supple body twined comfortably in the chair as she read from the book his mother had received as a wedding anniversary gift, shortly before she had died.

It was strange to see the daughter of his enemy giving his father so much pleasure. She was probably reading with her usual passionate expression and involvement, because his father looked relaxed and happy.

He thought how sweet she'd been when she'd fed chocolate cake to his father, administering to him without any hint of condescension or distaste. In fact her manner had been totally natural and easy and her conversation liberally sprinkled with anecdotes and humour.

Most people found it difficult being around his father. She seemed to know what to say and how to behave and that had touched him more than he could have thought possible.

Carmen ambled into the courtyard with the wheelchair to collect his father, and Jude slipped back into his room out of sight as Taz stood up to help.

He got ready for bed, feeling as if a part of him was missing. He smiled and checked his body wryly. Everything still there, plus assorted fading bruises. Resigned to taking it easy, he drew on a pair of cream silk pyjama bottoms and slung a silk dressing gown around his shoulders.

Restlessly he prowled around for a good hour, wondering what Taz was doing. And then he heard her in the room next door. Deliberately he slammed his wardrobe door, feeling as impatient as a child for her to pay him some attention.

But he'd missed her, really missed her.

He stood there in shock, staring into space.

There was a knock on the intervening door and then Taz burst in. She rushed over to where he stood, stunned into immobility by his discovery, and she caught hold of his arms, gazing anxiously into his stupefied face.

'What is it?' she cried breathlessly.

Slowly he bent his head, his brain dazed as it grappled with what was happening to him. She gave a fearful cry and said something but his head was roaring. He cared for her. Cared about her.

'Jude! Oh, God! Tell me! What is it?' she whispered.

He focussed. Her eyes were full of tears, the dark lashes sparkling with them. She cared too. OK, only because she thought he was ill, but he'd settle for Florence and Patient for a while.

In wonder he gently placed his hands on her small waist. Her ribcage heaved up and down beneath his palms. She seemed very upset. He inhaled slowly, closing his eyes as the essence of her came to him: clean, fresh, sweet and warm.

'That's it. Deep breathing,' she said. His heart was touched by the way she was trying to control her anxiety and speak normally. 'Now. What is it, Jude?'

'This,' he said helplessly, and kissed her very softly.

Her mouth felt soft and pliable, the faintest taste of salty tears tantalising his taste buds. She seemed to melt into his arms, her hands slipping to his neck and dislodging the robe as she returned the kiss. Her body was firm and cushioned against his bare chest and her heart beat fiercely like a muffled drum. For a moment he was in heaven and then she jerked, gave a cry and moved back.

'Taz—'

'You—you're not well!' she cried, her eyes huge and appalled. 'You don't know what you're doing. The drugs. Reaction.' She stared at his naked chest. Her arm flailed in explanation and Jude swiftly caught a small figurine as it flew from its resting place on the bureau. 'Oh! I'm sorry. I—you ought to be in bed. I mean…'

He took pity on her. 'Yes, Taz,' he said, not very successfully concealing his hoarseness. His hand went to his forehead. 'I—I don't know what happened to me,' he said truthfully. 'Will you stay and have dinner with me up here? In case I feel…odd again?'

He was being something of a fraud. But he had felt odd. Crazy. Ready to promise her the earth if she'd stay with him for…a long time. Longer than the brief marriage he'd envisaged. And that wasn't normal. He had no intention of getting sweet over her, however good her bedside manner. Or even despite it.

Damn the drugs.

'Jude!'

'What?'

'I was saying that you should get into bed now and I'll send down for our meals. Do you need help?'

Because she stood there biting her lip—an appealing action which made him long to rush forward and kiss her again—he assumed she didn't want to touch him right now.

'I can manage,' he muttered throatily.

She disappeared into her room until their meals arrived on trays. Jude sat up in bed wishing he didn't feel so weak. They ate in silence, other than the occasional polite request for seasoning or to remark on the tenderness of the chicken. The atmosphere felt laden with sexual tension and Jude knew that it would only be a matter of time before he felt well enough to make love to her. It had to be.

His face darkened and he put down his fork. He didn't like the idea of deceiving her. But how else could he fulfil his father's dreams?

Her hand came to his forehead. He looked at her and saw how gentle and concerned she was.

'I'm worried about you,' she said quietly. 'I'm not sure this wasn't a mistake, letting you out of hospital—'

He took her hand and kissed each fingertip before he knew what he was doing. 'I'm fine. Tired, that's all.' He put his tray on the table beside his bed. 'I've had enough. And you've hardly touched anything.'

'I'm not hungry,' she said quietly.

'You bother me,' he murmured.

'I do?' she croaked.

Her incomparable eyes rounded, her mouth too. Close to kissing her, he said quickly, 'You've chosen to work in a caring profession. You're kind and gentle, thoughtful and unselfish. That doesn't fit with a woman who regards casual sex as her right.'

She looked horrified. It was time to put him straight. 'I don't! You were my first and only lover! I adored you, Jude. I thought we were made for each other and you broke my heart.'

'But you indicated that you hadn't loved me,' he said carefully, watching her intently.

'I know. I just wanted to salvage my silly pride. There's…there's been no one else in my life since you left.'

His eyes seemed suddenly very bright. 'Oh, Taz!' he said huskily. 'You fool. You sweet idiot. Come here,' he said softly, holding out his arms to her.

'I—I know it was stupid to pretend I didn't care!' she said, finding herself somehow curled up on the bed and mumbling into his bare shoulder. 'But you were so cold and distant. I had to protect myself somehow—'

'It's OK,' he soothed, kissing her neck. He lay back on the pillows and cradled her in a close embrace, dropping little kisses on her forehead. 'I wasn't straight with you either. I did love you. Leaving you was the hardest thing I'd ever done.'

She scrambled up to look him in the face and he stroked her silky cheek in contrition. 'Then why—?'

'I couldn't continue to see you. You must see that.'

'You could have explained—!'

'You might have convinced me to stay with you. I knew I must not let that happen so I had to convince myself and you that our relationship had meant nothing.'

'You did convince me,' she said forlornly.

'Please understand. Denying my feelings was the only thing I could think of that would sever our relationship once and for all. I was poleaxed when my father had his stroke. He was in such a bad state that I was afraid he'd die if I told him I still cared for you.'

'So you dumped me for his sake,' she said soberly.

Jude raked a hand through his hair, his face harrowed. 'You supported your father. You refused to believe that I had no part in the affair. That hurt, Taz. Without trust there could be no future for us.'

'No,' she mumbled. 'That's true.'

His eyes blazed with memories. 'When I came to find your father I wanted to punish him for ruining my life, for taking away my happiness. God knows what I would have done if he'd been there.'

Her eyes were like bruises in her pale face. 'You took it out on me instead,' she whispered.

He lowered his gaze, the black lashes thick curves on his high cheekbones. 'Frustrated anger and misery overwhelmed me. I'm sorry. I'm so sorry,' he breathed hoarsely.

She clung to him tightly, folded in his arms, aching with the thought of what might have been. Mateo was entirely to blame and yet he was only to be pitied now.

'Stay with me,' Jude breathed. 'Lie beside me. I don't want to let you go.'

Beneath her hands, the power of his muscles rippled as he shifted to give her more space. But she remained stiff and silent. She wouldn't be used, not even by the man she loved. He might care, he might not, and she had no way of knowing. He was certainly frustrated. The hectic drumming of his pulses and the hard ridge throbbing against her thigh told her that.

But she couldn't trust him. As far as he knew, she owned half of the Laker hospital. And she was, therefore, an attractive proposition.

'This isn't right,' she muttered, easing away a little. 'It's not part of my duties.'

'What about comforting the patient?'

'There are limits,' she muttered.

'I'm glad to hear it,' he said in amusement. 'I'd hate to think you're as friendly with everyone you nurse. People would be queuing up for treatment.'

Gratefully she accepted the way out he'd offered her and took up his teasing tone.

'In that case I'll learn to scowl a lot, to ensure the wards are free of impediments—like sick people,' she said brightly. 'I've always thought that hospitals would run more smoothly without ill people about.'

'You couldn't be nasty if you tried,' he said tenderly. He

held her flushed face between the palms of his hands and gently kissed her.

'I could. Especially if you keep doing that,' she complained shakily.

'Then sleep well,' he said, releasing her with evident reluctance. 'I'm damned if I will.'

In the night, as she tossed and turned, her body hot with unsatisfied longing, she wondered if she'd made the wrong decision. But by the time she showered the next morning she'd come to the conclusion that she wanted a man who desired her and her alone. Jude wanted her half of the hospital.

'Hello, celibacy!' she said wryly to her doleful reflection.

And yet she burned, a moistness lubricating the most sensitive part of her body and challenging her to ignore her sexual arousal if she could.

Every day, being with Jude accelerated her frustration. It seemed that his body exuded an irresistible, musky allure that drew her dangerously close before her self-protective instincts took over and drove her into 'brisk nurse' mode.

They often laughed and joked and then the mood would change and she'd find herself melting from the effect of his velvety voice as he talked to her about La Quinta, his eyes soft and liquid with love for his home. She wanted that love. She wanted those sensual tones to be directed to her, not a building and its land, however beautiful they might be.

Quite quickly she came to know the land well: the huge glasshouses of exotic flowers for the hotel and leisure industry; the rich farmland which produced an abundance of crops; and cool, aromatic woodland.

Jude had put his heart and soul into the land, working far into the night to make it viable. Her admiration for him grew too profound for her peace of mind and she had the feeling that she was tumbling willingly towards a disaster.

People called: no one dripping in jewels and cut-glass accents, but men and women at ease with themselves who seemed genuinely interested in Jude, his father, life in general...and her. Far from being awed by them, she could be herself, and she marvelled that his friends could be so relaxed and friendly.

He told her that he believed a rich life came from a loving family, good food and wine and strong friendships, and the best of these were free. She agreed. Sitting in the candlelit garden, chatting to his friends after a good meal, was blissful.

The days sped by too quickly. Soon she must speak to Jude and then it would be time to go. But it would be a wrench to leave. The magic of La Quinta had won her heart.

And she craved the caresses Jude denied her with an increasing desperation, almost angry with him for containing his evident lust—even though she would have preferred his love, not his desire.

Today he'd mysteriously told her that he was taking her somewhere special. She took a white sundress she hadn't worn before from the heavily carved wardrobe and placed it on the bed. He'd like it, she thought, and then flushed because she knew she wanted him to find her totally irresistible.

'I'm an idiot! What am I going to do, Graham?' she whispered hopelessly.

Accidentally her hand brushed her firm honey-gold stomach. Tentatively she tried to feel what he'd feel if he ever touched her again. Slowly her fingers glided over the smooth skin and curved around the soft swell of her hip. There he'd encounter a scrap of white silk, a fragile barrier...

Taz gulped, her eyes huge. Blocking out his next inevitable step, she glanced at the full-length mirror to see what he'd see. A woman with a mass of dark hair seductively sweeping over one eye. An unmistakable look of desire. Pouting, parted lips, white teeth, breasts spilling from their beautifully cut silk bra, each nipple long and dark as if begging for his mouth.

She swallowed again, overcome by an irrepressible ache.

'Taz! Hurry up! Are you there?' he shouted from outside her door.

Oh, yes, I'm there, she thought ruefully. 'Just a minute!' she yelled back and frantically hauled the dress over her head. In her mind she was there, in his arms, locked in an intimate embrace.

'I'm leaving in five minutes!' he called.

And she would be leaving him very soon. Pain contorted her face and her body twitched from a sharp spasm of anguish. She reached for the hairbrush and began to sweep her hair back off her face. It had to be today. She would put the proposition to him. Her throat tightened.

She gazed at the hoyden in the mirror and asked herself, Which proposition? because all she could think of was making love with him. Impatient with herself, she threw the brush down, slipped her feet into a pair of low sandals and ran out, her loose hair sliding sensually over her shoulders.

And never had she felt so sexy and reckless. She was unnervingly eager to court danger, to give herself to Jude. And she didn't know whether she was afraid or elated at the prospect.

CHAPTER NINE

JUDE gasped when he saw her at the top of the huge staircase. If Carmen hadn't been standing beside him he would have hurtled up the stairs towards her and carried her, willing or not, to his bedroom. No. He didn't mean that He wanted her uninhibited surrender.

As it was, he held onto his sanity by the skin of his teeth. Women as well-endowed as Taz shouldn't run. The movement of her breasts was seriously endangering his health. She looked more beautiful, more desirable than ever.

'Thought you'd never come,' he growled, dragging his gaze away. His hand went to Carmen's shoulder. 'You will be all right for a while? You can manage?'

'I'll get by.' She smiled fondly. 'Enjoy your day, Don Judeo. Don't catch cold.'

'With the temperature in the eighties, I'm not likely to,' he said, his necessarily stern expression softening.

Carmen winked. 'You never know,' she said airily, tapping her nose. 'The sun is hot. You get heated and take off your clothes and then you're chilled. It's happened to me. Happens all the time.'

Jude frowned. Surely she wasn't suggesting...? Carmen chuckled and shuffled away, muttering to herself. Taz ended up a few feet away from him, the scent of woman driving his sensory nerves crazy.

'Come on,' he muttered.

'Sorry I'm late,' she said breathlessly.

He risked shooting her a glance as they walked out to the car. Her face was flushed and her eyes were sparkling. There was a glow to her skin and she looked so carefree that his heart missed a beat.

He smiled down at her apologetic face, melting before all that sweet sensuality. 'It's OK. I was impatient.' That didn't sound right. 'I wanted you to see something before it got too late in the day.'

'Intriguing,' she said huskily.

Even sitting beside her in the car seemed different today. He'd been highly aware of her before but this time he was certain that she wanted him with equal intensity. His throat tightened and he could hardly breathe.

The electricity seemed to crackle between them and he drove with exaggerated care because his mind kept being diverted every time Taz drew in a breath and the thin cotton fabric strained against her fabulous breasts.

She crossed her legs. He crashed a gear. She uncrossed them. His hands gripped the steering wheel tightly as he manoeuvred the car towards his goal.

Towards the place where he'd seduce her.

He stopped on a low hill and let the scenery do its job. Satisfyingly, she gasped and leaned forward, then flung open the car door and jumped out for a better view of the flower meadows.

With ferocious lust, he confined himself to a different view. Taz: her hair fluttering in the wind, her face lifted to the perfumed breeze, perfect body held proudly. The skirts of her dress swirled around her long, bare brown legs, offering an occasional tantalising glimpse of firm golden thigh.

'It's fabulous!' she cried, turning back to him in awe.

Jude managed to ease himself out of the car. He strolled slowly to her, affecting nonchalance to cover his restricted movement.

Below lay a tapestry of colour: seemingly oceans of violet and turquoise, saffron and rose, where clover, buttercup, cranesbill, camomile and orchid fields stretched in glorious array.

'What do you do with these fields?' she breathed, her eyes wide and as dark as the lake at midnight.

'Look at them. Enjoy them.' Shaken by her soft mouth, he gazed at the coloured carpet, which was being ruffled by the same wind which carried her heat to him. 'I bring Father here. We just sit and marvel.'

'You're very good to him,' she said soberly. 'And to all your staff. They think the world of you.'

He turned her around and held her shoulders, looking deeply into her eyes. 'That's because they trust me. They know I'm honest and reliable. I wish you felt like that too.'

'I—I want to believe in you, but...'

'You daren't.'

Her face suddenly miserable, she heaved a huge sigh. 'It doesn't matter. My feelings are irrelevant. Jude, you're well enough to manage now. It's time I left, so—'

'I don't want you to go!' he cried urgently, holding her more tightly. 'Taz,' he whispered more softly. 'I don't want you to go.'

Her troubled eyes were almost liquid. 'How can I stay?' she said jerkily. 'You don't need me—'

'But I do!' he broke in hotly. He wanted to tell her why, but chickened out and found several other reasons. 'You know Carmen is racked with arthritis. You've been keeping an eye on her, as well as Father. Carmen can't take care of him any longer. You're needed here more than ever.'

Her disappointment was immense. For a moment his re-action had been so instant and so passionate that she'd imag-ined he wanted her for himself. But she had other uses: as a nurse to his old nanny and his father!

She tore away and hurried down the hill. 'Leave me alone!' she shouted petulantly when he followed, feeling like stamping her foot like a cross child.

'I can't!' he growled.

He strode to her and pulled her around, groaning at the lush sensation as her supple body collided with his.

'Jude!' she whispered in shock.

Tormented beyond reason, he took that open mouth in a

deep and ruthless kiss, smothering her protests. 'You mustn't leave because I want you,' he muttered urgently.

His fingers slid aside the slender straps of her bodice and his mouth roamed freely over the pulsing warmth of her skin. To his delight, she uttered little moans of pleasure and her body melted into his, the hardness of her nipples exciting him beyond all measure.

'Kiss me again,' she said huskily, taking his face between her hands.

Her mouth was open and moist. A kick of raw hunger ripped through his body as he tasted her and she shuddered, lifting one leg and hooking it over his hip.

He muttered her name, his brain ceasing to function as he kissed her and bent his head to suckle her swollen breasts. Unable to wait any longer, he slid his hands beneath her skirt, his fingers moving over a small triangle of silk that covered her high, rounded buttocks. He shut his eyes, revelling in their sensuous shape, cupping the two globes firmly before ripping the silk in one, frantic movement just as she tore apart his shirt and placed her mouth on his hard, taut nipple.

The sensation rocked him. He bore her to the ground, crushing clover and sweet herbs, stroking her until she arched her body and began to beg for release.

'Make love to me!' she breathed harshly.

He hovered above her, worshipping her body with his eyes, a strange feeling welling up inside him. Tentatively he touched her, his fingers rubbing gently at her moistness and exploring her warmth. Almost as if in a dream, he undressed her and she tenderly removed his clothes, kissing him slowly and passionately as she did so.

She knelt there, gloriously golden amongst the deep-pink clover, and her hand gently glided over his hard, aching shaft. It was unbearable. He pushed her back and she crowed with delight, her legs lifting around his back as he drove into her.

The pleasure seemed to last a lifetime. He was conscious only of their movement, her tight heat around him, the feel of her body beneath his and the pressure of their mouths fighting in an urgent, wanton frenzy.

This is it, he thought hazily, as his body screamed to a higher and higher level of ecstasy. More than sex. More than obsession, domination, revenge, infatuation. Love. I love her. I don't ever want this to stop. Ever want her to go. Must keep her. Mine. *Mine.*

He began to cry out, the truth too overwhelming to keep inside him. 'Taz!' he muttered gutturally. 'Taz,' he croaked.

'I love you,' she whispered, her voice high and reedy.

Something crashed like exploding stars in his mind. She loved him. Now. This minute. A whirling heat took hold of his entire nervous system as she gasped beneath him and cried out his name.

Slowly he began to slide off the pinnacle of pleasure and his brain kicked in. That was how it felt. Making love to someone you felt a profound and intense love for. Incredible. Mind-blowing. More intense, powerful, seismic than he could have imagined possible.

He felt his heart racing and opened his eyes. Taz was sleepily smiling at him, love in every line of her face.

'I love you, Taz,' he confessed hoarsely and he kissed her startled mouth, laughing when she spluttered and tried to push him away, begging for an explanation. 'It's simple,' he breathed, nibbling her ear. 'I love you. And I'd do that again, now, if I thought I could, but I need to recover—'

'Jude!' she cried loudly in his ear. 'Sorry!' she giggled, when he winced. 'It's just that…are you all right? I mean, your head, your heart—'

'I feel wonderful. Fantastic.'

'You're shaking—'

'Arnold Schwarzenegger would be shaking after that!' A small doubt crept into his mind. 'You prefer me to be ill? You like playing nursemaid?' he muttered.

'Oh, no! I want you to be well more than anything in the world,' she said fervently. 'It's been my most passionate wish and I can't wait till you're totally recovered.'

The worry vanished, taking with it the frown line between his lowered brows. For a long time he lay with her in the warm sunshine, soaking up the heat into his naked body. They sat up to watch the sunset and he tenderly dressed her, remarking with mock horror that she'd have to return without any briefs and that all the buttons on his shirt had been ripped from the cloth.

'I have something to give you,' he murmured, when they'd sneaked, giggling, into a side door of the house and had reached the safety of Jude's bedroom. He took the two long ropes of Corderro pearls from their box in the wall safe. 'These belong to the family. They're priceless. Sit on the bed, Taz, so I can put them on you.'

'No, Jude!' she gasped. 'You can't do that! I—' She felt upset. What was he trying to do, trying to prove? 'They should stay in the family. F-for your bride,' she stumbled.

His eyes commanded her. 'Sit!' he said, pointing to the bed.

'We both know the score,' she said soberly. 'You'll marry someone aristocratic and suitable, like Isabel—'

He threw back his head and roared with laughter. 'Isabel? Taz, you dolt, hasn't anyone seen fit to tell you? She's not aristocratic, she's my farm manager's daughter! I'm putting her through college because she's clever and wants to follow in his footsteps. Don't you know me well enough by now? Am I a snob? Don't I—and all Andalusians—treat people from all walks of life as equals? Money and position come and go. It is honour that I value. I want you to have the pearls. Please.'

Honour, she thought sadly. It would always come between them. But how could she resist his honeyed, coaxing tones? Mulling over what he'd said, she obeyed.

He lifted her legs and swung them around so that she was

lying on the bed and then his mouth was on hers, moving gently and insistently.

She sighed dreamily and then became aware of something coiled around each wrist. Her eyes snapped open and Jude sat back in triumph as she looked from side to side and discovered that the two ropes of pearls were fastened around her wrists and had been looped over the carved lion heads on the bed head.

'What...?' she whispered.

'You must not move,' he murmured huskily. 'Or the pearls will break and be ruined.'

Taz drew in a sharp breath, unbearably excited by the dangerous look in his eyes and the contemplative smile on his sensual mouth. An answering, sultry smile parted her own lips.

'You're very wicked, Jude Corderro,' she said reprovingly.

'Lie still. Enjoy,' he growled.

Taz shut her eyes and surrendered to her senses. Jude's fingers massaged her scalp slowly and methodically and all the while her body was screaming to be touched.

She encouraged him to do so with little moans and pleas and by writhing her hips. He ignored everything she did and concentrated on stroking her face, inch by inch, and then, when her skin tingled, he followed his feathering touch with light kisses.

'Stop now,' she moaned as his tongue flickered around her sensitised mouth.

'But I've only just begun.'

Carefully he unzipped her dress and slid it down her body. Her bra he unhooked and lifted away, hurling both items over his shoulder. When he dragged off his torn shirt she saw that his eyes were glazed, his chest heaving. His mouth came down, warm and searching on her neck and throat, then travelled inexorably over every inch of her body.

And she dared not move. It was an exquisite torture.

Sometimes she'd give a little flinch and whimper with pleasure but mostly she was forced to contain her reaction to his slow and intense lovemaking. As her eyes flickered and dimmed with the drugging desire he became a blur of dark hair curling damply on his forehead, dark eyes, murmuring mouth and golden body.

Then her whole being seemed suffused with pleasure-filled nerves, her mind and emotions abandoning themselves to hedonism as Jude slid the pearls from her wrists and caressed her lovingly. She could feel the warm liquid of the core of her body welcoming him, taking him in and tightening around him. She began to thrust with him, some primal urge taking over from her paralysed brain.

Raw. Basic. Total.

They were crying out together, rolling with one another over the bed, grappling in a frenzy of arms and legs, mouths, tongues, scrabbling hands. Spasm after spasm rocked them, Jude's grunts and her gasps sending hot, sweet spurts of breath into one another's mouth. She seemed to climb some extraordinary peak of pleasure, tremble upon it for a long, protracted moment, and then drift down into a shuddering, sighing softness.

I love him more than my own life, she thought muzzily. And slid into a deep and dreamless sleep.

They showered together later, and wandered hand in hand down to the vaulted dining room for dinner. But she began to feel edgy. There was unfinished business between them.

'You've dropped your fork twice now,' he eventually said quietly. 'What's the matter?'

Carefully she put her hands in her lap. They were trembling. She raised huge eyes to his. This was the moment she'd dreaded.

'You want the hospital, don't you?'

His expression sobered immediately. 'Yes,' he said after a long, heart-stopping time.

Taz nodded. 'Bel and I have agreed that you can buy into

it as a partner.' She named the sum. Jude didn't react but stared at her as if she were a volatile explosive he wasn't sure how to handle. 'It's what you want,' she whispered through dry lips. 'You'll own fifty-five per cent of the equity. That gives you the casting vote. It'll be virtually yours.'

'Why?' he asked quietly.

She looked down, staring at her shaking hands blindly. This would test him. He'd either laugh and say the hospital could go under or he'd greedily accept her offer. What then? Suddenly she felt as if the ground was falling away from under her. He said he loved her but revenge was the first thing on his mind.

Taz gave a small, stifled sob. 'Because it's bankrupt.'

He stiffened. 'How long have you known?'

'A—a week or so, perhaps longer—'

'Before you agreed to nurse me here?' he shot. 'Was that why you accepted so readily,' he spat, 'because you thought you'd use me to salvage your precious father's hospital?'

'I—I… Yes. Partly, but—'

'Thanks, Taz!' He flung down his napkin and jerked from his seat so violently that the tooled-leather chair fell back with a crash. 'Now I know where I stand,' he scathed. 'I thought you wanted me, not my money. I should have realised you were operating another honey-trap—'

'No!' she yelled, leaping up in fury. 'You're *wrong*! You must believe me, Jude, you must!'

His eyes burned, his mouth was wrenched into a vicious snarl. 'Don't, Taz!' he blazed. 'I've had enough of your family! First your father destroys my father's life, then your stepmother lures me into marriage and now you seduce me with your doe eyes and sweet nature and loving words…' He sucked in a juddering breath. 'And all for this—this useless, bankrupt *folly*!'

Taz stared, her senses reeling. 'Wait a minute!' Excitedly she ran to Jude, who backed away, his hands held out protectively.

'Get away from me!' he growled. 'I want nothing to do with you! You won't ruin my life—'

'Listen, will you?' she yelled, slipping beneath his arms and beating her fists against his chest. 'It's about Bel! Why was she so sure you'd agree to marry her?'

He gave an impatient snort of contempt. 'Because I want the hospital, that's why!' he snapped irritably.

'But how did she know that?' she cried in triumph.

His face changed. One moment it was full of fury and anguish and the next it was frozen in bewilderment. Taz tried to calm herself down. Something didn't add up and she was sure it was important.

'Perhaps,' Jude said slowly, 'someone told her. Your father?'

'Possibly.' Taz's mind raced. There was only one other person who could have been aware of Jude's interest. 'Harvey!' she cried excitedly. 'He's been working for the hospital since it opened. He was Father's legal assistant, Jude!'

'What?' She had his whole attention now.

'He knew where you and your father lived,' she said breathlessly. 'Doesn't that suggest he knew more about you than one would expect? And…he said that once he'd done something dreadful, which he now regretted—'

Jude let out a sharp expletive. 'Where will he be at this time of night?' he asked grimly.

'Maybe still at the hospital—'

'Let's *go!*'

She drove skilfully and with the utmost concentration down the mountain road, knowing Jude was fretting because he wasn't allowed to drive on the public highway yet.

They raced into the hospital and Jude flung open Harvey's door in a dramatic movement, his eyes dark and glittering beneath his lowered brows and every line of his body more menacing than Taz would have believed possible.

'I will invest heavily in this hospital,' he said in a low,

threatening tone, 'only if you tell me what you know. Why, for instance, do you imagine I'd be interested? How do you know I'm interested? What link is there between you and David Laker—?'

'OK. OK!' Harvey sat down shakily, wiping his sweating face, and waved them both to a seat which neither of them accepted. 'I've wanted to tell you for a long time, Taz,' he said hoarsely. 'I've felt bad about it—'

'Just get to the point,' snapped Jude.

Harvey swallowed. 'David Laker was a crook.'

Jude's glance slanted to Taz. She looked as white as a sheet. He pushed her to a seat and held her hand firmly. 'Go on,' he said coldly.

'I'm sorry, Taz,' Harvey said. 'Bel had said she wanted you to have only the best memories of your father—'

'It doesn't work, keeping things from people,' she said in a forlorn voice. 'I discovered that when I tried to protect Bel.'

Harvey looked miserable. As well he might. Jude felt a roaring in his ears as Harvey told Taz about the scam David Laker had carefully set up. In return for acting as legal advisor in the deal, Harvey had been guaranteed a plum job at the hospital and a golden future.

'We set up a complicated system so that Mateo Corderro's investment could be "lost". Then I tore up all the documents relating to Corderro's investment,' Harvey said unhappily. 'I was then able to swear that no such documents existed. Your father had the money and total control of the hospital. But…the hospital rightfully belongs to the Corderro family and I'll stand up in court and say that if you want me to.'

Taz was reeling from shock. 'Do you remember that time we talked about this in the staffroom? I asked you *directly* whether Mateo was telling the truth during the trial!' she said angrily. 'You *lied* to me, Harvey—and you *lied* under oath in court. How *could* you?'

'I'm sorry.' He looked broken, full of despair. 'Lying in court wasn't a problem. But lying to you was the hardest thing I've ever done. I was afraid I'd lose my job…' There was a long pause while Jude scowled ferociously at Harvey. 'I'll clear my desk,' he mumbled.

'Do that!' Jude's words came out like a pistol crack. 'And don't show your face again—'

'Oh, Harvey! Take care of Bel!' Taz said shakily.

'I will. I love her. We're happy—'

'Leave!' Jude growled. 'Taz—'

She was in tears. Jude jerked his head at Harvey, who swiftly left the room. Kneeling down, Jude tenderly held her in his embrace, allowing her to sob on his shoulder, her tears racking her body with a violence that brought him close to tears too.

'I wish you didn't have to find out about your father like this,' he said gently.

'I—I kind of knew. If I'd had any sense I would have picked up on the clues. But I didn't want to know, Jude! I'm sorry!' she wailed. 'I'll never forgive myself! I've made the most awful mistake, a terrible mess of things—'

'It doesn't matter now,' he murmured, kissing her wet face reverently. 'We have the truth now. It was all I ever wanted. My father is vindicated. And I love you, Taz. That's all that's important, isn't it?'

'Wha-a-a-t?' she mumbled, blowing her nose on the linen handkerchief he handed to her. 'You can't! Not now, I mean—' She jumped up in agitation and to his delight her arm swept in an arc across Harvey's desk, bringing everything to the floor: telephone, papers, diary, pens, keys…all making a resounding crash as they hit the elegant parquet flooring.

'I think I'd better take you home,' he said gently.

Her eyes filled with tears again. 'I haven't got a home!' she sniffed.

'Yes, you have. La Quinta. I'm not having my wife living anywhere else.'

'W-wife?'

'I love you, you love me. You know I wasn't involved in deceit, I know you were unaware of your father's fraud and that you didn't know he was encouraging you to befriend me. So you're not a conniving little madam and so therefore we must get married.'

'Must?' she repeated, looking dazed.

'Darling,' he murmured, taking advantage of her and kissing her long and slow. 'If we don't, Graham, for one, will be appalled.'

'I want a better proposal than that,' she protested, her mouth curving beautifully.

'Get me home and you'll have it,' he promised, his heart racing. And he kissed her again. 'You'll have roses and champagne, strawberries, sweet words and music—'

'Chocolate,' she said firmly.

'Anywhere in particular?' he asked innocently.

'All of those,' she breathed, her face lovely in its happiness, 'all over me. You included.'

'I'll have to blindfold Graham,' he murmured and, to his joy, she laughed. He would see that she didn't suffer too badly from discovering that her father had deceived her. He'd wrap her in love and protect her from all harm and she could be Florence at the hospital if she so wanted. 'Home,' he said gently.

She smiled, starry-eyed. 'Home.'

Mateo watched them from the balcony of his quarters, locked together in the flickering light of candles beneath a black velvet sky. Vying with the whirring cicadas, the love duet from Puccini's *Madame Butterfly* drifted out from the music centre in Jude's study.

Mateo's heart seemed to be bursting with joy. Jude, his beloved and loyal son, had finally cleared the family name.

And Taz, the dear delightful girl he'd always adored, was to be his daughter-in-law. Everyone loved her, especially the cheery young American she'd chosen to be his nurse. The whole of La Quinta was in a whirl preparing for the wedding and he couldn't have been happier.

A lump came to his throat as he saw them draw apart and gaze at one another as if mesmerised. He remembered himself as a young man, smiling into the eyes of a woman as sweet, funny and as good as Taz. Memories… He had so many—but there would be more to come: the wedding, his first grandchild…

He sighed happily. Maybe he was locked within his body. But he could still see and feel and love, his senses more acute than ever. And he would not have missed these beautiful days, or the days to come, for anything.

Tenderly Jude kissed Taz's small, upturned face and Mateo closed his eyes to allow them privacy. The image remained with him: Jude, tall and powerful, protectively enclosing Taz's loveliness in his arms.

Far beyond, the snow on the Sierras would be melting and the high pastures would burst into colour as gentians, crocuses and narcissi emerged. It was a time of hope and the dynasty was safe. They'd have many babies. What a joy a loving family could bring! he thought, and with a smile of deep contentment he let himself slip into a profoundly happy sleep.

The world's bestselling romance series.

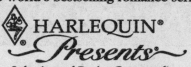

HARLEQUIN® Presents·

Seduction and Passion Guaranteed!

INTERNATIONAL
DOCTORS

They're guaranteed to raise your pulse!

**Meet the most eligible medical men of the world,
in a new series of stories, by popular authors,
that will make your heart race!**

**Whether they're saving lives or dealing with desire,
our doctors have got bedside manners that
send temperatures soaring....**

Coming in Harlequin Presents in 2003:

**Pick up a Harlequin Presents® novel and you will enter a world
of spine-tingling passion and provocative, tantalizing romance!**

Available wherever Harlequin books are sold.

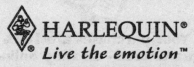

HARLEQUIN®
Live the emotion™

Visit us at www.eHarlequin.com

HPINTDOC

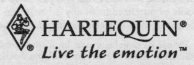

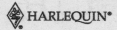

The world's bestselling romance series.

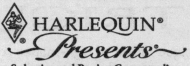

Seduction and Passion Guaranteed!

Miranda Lee...
Emma Darcy...
Helen Bianchin...
Lindsay Armstrong...

Some of our bestselling writers are Australians!

Look out for their novels about the Wonder of Down Under—where spirited women win the hearts of Australia's most eligible men.

Don't miss
The Billionaire's Contract Bride
by **Carol Marinelli**, #2372
On sale in January 2004

Pick up a Harlequin Presents® novel and you will enter a world of spine-tingling passion and provocative, tantalizing romance!

Available wherever Harlequin books are sold.

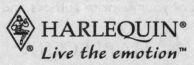

Visit us at www.eHarlequin.com

HPAUSJ04

HARLEQUIN®
INTRIGUE®

Our unique brand of high-caliber romantic
suspense just cannot be contained. And to meet
our readers' demands, Harlequin Intrigue is
expanding its publishing schedule
to include **SIX** breathtaking titles
every month!

Check out the new lineup
in October!

MORE variety.
MORE pulse-pounding excitement.
MORE of your favorite authors and series.

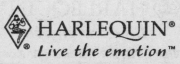

HARLEQUIN®
Live the emotion™

Visit us at www.tryIntrigue.com

HI4T06T

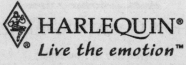